CHILDREN'S DOCTOR, SOCIETY BRIDE

BY
JOANNA NEIL

MILLS & BOON
Pure reading pleasure™

All the characters in this book have no existence outside the imagination of the author, and have no relation whatsoever to anyone bearing the same name or names. They are not even distantly inspired by any individual known or unknown to the author, and all the incidents are pure invention.

First published in Great Britain 2008
Paperback edition 2009
Harlequin Mills & Boon Limited,
Eton House, 18-24 Paradise Road, Richmond, Surrey TW9 1SR

© Joanna Neil 2008

ISBN: 978 0 263 86823 4

Set in Times Roman 10½ on 13 pt
03-0209-46766

Printed and bound in Spain
by Litografia Rosés, S.A., Barcelona

CHILDREN'S DOCTOR, SOCIETY BRIDE

CHAPTER ONE

'JUST try to take a drop more for me, cherub.' Louise gently brushed the teat of the bottle against the baby's lips and smiled as he began to suckle once more. 'That's the way…that's good,' she murmured softly. 'You need to build up your strength, little one.' Smiling, she leaned back in her chair, nestling the baby in her arms, rocking gently to and fro.

'He's doing well, isn't he, considering that he's recovering from emergency heart surgery?' Alice, the specialist nurse, came to peer down at her precious bundle.

'He is.' Louise nodded agreement, and then looked up at Alice with a wry smile. 'I suppose you've come to take him away from me, have you?'

'I have, I'm afraid.' Her dark hair made a silky swathe as she nodded. 'His mother's talking to the surgeon, and I want to have all my observations recorded before she comes back. The doctor's bound to want to take another look at him, and I need to make sure that he's ready.'

Louise gave a soft sigh. 'Ah, well, he's finished off all of his milk, so I guess I have no excuse for keeping him to myself any longer.'

She winded the baby, lightly rubbing his back until he gave a soft burp, and then she reluctantly handed the infant over to Alice's care. Getting to her feet, she flicked back her shoulder-length auburn hair with a deft twist of her fingers.

'Thanks for letting me steal him for a few minutes. I can't resist coming over here to the paediatric ward whenever I have a few minutes to spare. It was lovely to be able to sit here and relax for a while. It's been so hectic in the children's A&E this morning that I was glad of a chance to come and wind down for a bit.'

'I can imagine. Are you on call for the whole day?' Alice slid a thermometer into the baby's armpit and checked the monitor before noting down his pulse rate on to the chart.

Louise shook her head. 'It was just for this morning. I'm off to grab myself some lunch now, and then I have to conduct interviews this afternoon. We're looking for another Senior House Officer to take on some of the workload—though how that will pan out with all the hoo-ha that's been going on of late, I'm not entirely sure.'

Alice's grey eyes took on a sombre look. 'I can't believe that they'll go ahead with it. How can they even think of closing the unit down? What are people going to do if their children become desperately ill all at once or get knocked over by a car? The A&E at the

Royal Forest Hospital is almost forty miles away for some people in the outlying areas. And if they close down the children's A&E, the adult A&E here will go too. I can't believe that they've thought it through properly.'

'Neither can I. It makes me so angry when I think about it. We've been so fortunate in having a separate children's emergency unit here—in some places they are still combined with the adult unit. It's essential to have a department dedicated to children's A&E, with specialist staff, and yet now they plan to destroy everything.' Louise straightened up, her jaw setting in a tight angle. 'See, I'm getting fractious all over again. I shall have to go and eat lunch in the park just to calm myself down.'

'Have some for me. A crisp salad in a crusty bread roll, along with an ice-cold bottle of fruit juice would do just nicely.' Alice smiled before turning back to her small patient. Making a swift check of his nappy, she wrinkled her nose. 'Oh, we'll have to do something about that, won't we, pumpkin?'

'See you later, Alice.' Louise went in search of the lifts. The sooner she was out in the warm, fresh air of the park, surrounded by the green shade of trees and shrubs, the better.

How could they even think of taking her A&E unit from her? After all the work that had gone into building it up and making it the smooth running enterprise that it was today, it was nothing short of criminal to contemplate pulling the plug. What would happen to children who were grievously injured, or who were suffering from the onset of septicaemia if they had an hour-long journey ahead of them before they reached the skilled team workers in the A&E department at the Royal Forest Hospital?

She was still aggrieved when she reached the relative sanctuary of the local park. At least there, though, she could take solace in watching the gently flowing waters of the river as it meandered along the valley carved out through meadowland over the centuries. Broad trees that had stood the test of time spread their branches heavenward, and she looked up at the blue of the sky and basked for a moment in the gentle heat of the summer sun. This was just a small part of the beautiful Wye Valley, and she was eternally pleased that she had decided to make her home here.

Glancing around, she searched for a table where she might sit and eat her sandwiches. Not too far away, children were joyfully kicking a ball over the neatly cut grass and, closer to the water's edge, a young couple sat and followed the progress of swans as they glided gracefully beneath the arch of a stone bridge.

A little further in the distance, an elderly man was making his way slowly towards a large oak tree. A bench seat surrounded the massive trunk, and Louise guessed that the man was heading there with the bench in mind.

He was smartly dressed, wearing a suit and waistcoat, but as she looked closer it occurred to her that he didn't look at all well. He was coughing, she noticed, and his breath was coming in short bursts. As she drew closer to him, she could see that his lips were faintly blue.

'Are you all right?' she asked in a tentative voice, her green eyes troubled as she approached him. He must be in his eighties, and because of his frailty she was immediately worried about him. What on earth was he doing out here on his own? Surely someone ought to be looking out for him?

'I'm just a bit short of breath,' he managed. 'I'll be fine in a minute.'

'Were you trying to get over to the seat?' she asked, and he nodded. 'Perhaps I could help you, then?' she suggested, and when he acquiesced she lent a supporting arm so that he could lean on her.

Slowly, they covered the short distance to the bench and she steadied him as he lowered himself down onto the seat.

'Thank you,' he said, gasping for air as he finally leaned back against the trunk of the tree.

Louise sat down beside him. 'Just rest there for a while,' she said. 'You looked as though you were about to stumble. Were you feeling dizzy?'

He nodded, clearly unable to answer her right then. Sitting this close to him, she could hear the wheezing in his chest, and she frowned.

'Are you on any kind of medication?' she wondered. 'It's just that I'm a doctor and I can see that you're very pale, and it's clear that you were finding it difficult to go on.'

He put a shaky hand to his chest, patting his ribcage.

'The ticker's not all it used to be.' He began to fumble in his pockets, but Louise realised that he was struggling and intervened.

'Do you have some tablets that you need to take? Perhaps I could help you to find them?'

He made a weary inclination of his head. 'In my pocket,' he said.

'This one?' Louise carefully slid her hand into his jacket where he indicated, and drew out a small plastic bottle. She read the label. 'These are to slow your heart rate and lower your blood pressure,' she murmured. 'Would it be best for you to take one of these tablets now? I have a bottle of water on me.'

'Yes, thanks.' There was a hint of relief in his voice.

She opened the container and tipped a tablet into his palm, and then she unscrewed the lid off her water bottle and held it out to him. 'I'm sorry I don't have a cup,' she said. 'Will you manage?'

Again he tilted his head in acknowledgement, but she could see that he was still shaky, and so she helped him with the bottle and watched as he sipped some of the liquid, swallowing the tablet down.

'It will take a while for the medicine to work,' Louise murmured. 'You should just sit and rest for a while. You don't need to talk if it's difficult for you. Just take your time.'

She sat with him and he closed his eyes for a while. Later, when he appeared to have recovered a little, she said quietly, 'Is there anyone I can call who could come and take you home?'

'I was with my grandson,' he said, sucking in a ragged breath, his voice a little cracked with strain. 'We were having a cup of tea together in town, but he had to go off and make some phone calls.'

'And he didn't come back?'

He shook his head. 'I expect it was something important.'

Louise frowned. 'So...let me see if I have this right... You were with your grandson, but he left you on your own so that he could go and call someone?'

'No, they called him.'

'Oh, I see.' She didn't, not really, but at least the old gentleman seemed to be breathing a little more easily now, and Louise was pleased about that. Even so, he definitely wasn't well enough to be left on his own, and it was annoying to think that his own grandson could abandon him so casually.

'Do you have your grandson's number—presumably he has a mobile phone with him? I could give him a ring and ask him to come and fetch you.' She was already reaching for her phone.

'Um...yes, I think so.' Hesitantly, he supplied the number, and it occurred to Louise that he might be getting on in years, but his mind was still keen enough if he could recall the digits. 'His name is James,' he added.

'Okay.' Louise started to dial the number. She felt like giving James a piece of her mind for leaving his grandfather. What kind of person would go off without a care in the world and leave his grandfather to fend for himself?

The engaged tone started to bleep, and Louise felt her irritation begin to rise. She stabbed the button on her phone with her finger, shutting off the noise. What was the matter with the man? Was he so busy calling all and sundry that he had lost sight of everything else?

She tried not to let her annoyance show. 'He's talking on the phone,' she told the old man. 'I'll try him again in a minute or two.' She looked at him carefully. 'You seem to have a little more colour in your cheeks now,' she said. 'Are you feeling a bit better?'

'Yes, I am, thanks.' There was still an underlying rasp to his voice, and she guessed that his chest was badly congested. If he had been one of her patients, she would have asked to check out his lungs and his heart, and she would have taken a look at his ankles to see if there was any swelling there.

'Are you having regular check-ups at the hospital or with your GP?' she asked. 'Perhaps you ought to go and see someone fairly soon.'

He reached out and patted her hand. 'You're very kind,' he said, giving her a smile, 'but I'm getting on a bit these days, and there's probably not too much that anyone can do for me.'

'You won't know unless you ask.' She felt an immediate empathy towards this old gentleman. Now that he was feeling a little better, she could see that there was a faint twinkle in his eyes, and she guessed that he had been a lively soul in years gone by.

'I'll try your grandson again,' she said, deftly thumbing in the numbers once more.

This time, the ringing was answered after just a short time.

'Hello, James Ashleigh speaking.' The tone was concise, the voice a deep, masculine timbre that was easy on the ear.

'Hello. I'm so glad that I managed to reach you at last,' she began. 'I'm Louise Bridgford. I have your grandfather here with me, and I'm afraid he's not feeling too well. I wonder if you would care to come and fetch him?'

There was a pause on the other end of the line. 'What's wrong with him?'

'He's struggling for breath and he needed to sit down for a while.'

'Where are you?'

James was obviously a man of few words, and Louise decided to be equally succinct. 'We're in Castle Park, just about a quarter of a mile from the entrance.'

'I'll come and find you. Will you be able to stay with him until I get there?'

'I won't leave him on his own,' she said in a clipped voice. She was tempted to add, *unlike some*, but she managed to restrain herself. No doubt her sharp manner would have been enough to convey the message.

He cut the call, and for a moment she stared down at the blank screen. So much for James Ashleigh, grandson extraordinaire... How long was it going to take for him to get here? she wondered. Would he manage to avoid any detours or distractions along the way?

She turned her attention back to the man beside her. 'He's coming over,' she said.

He smiled broadly, his features relaxing properly for the first time since she had met him. 'That's good.' He glanced around. 'I don't think he's set foot in this park since he was a child,' he said on a musing note. 'We used to bring him here, his grandmother and me. Those were good times.'

Louise's mouth curved. 'I can imagine.' They talked for a while about those visits and the way the riverside had always been an attractive spot for picnics. Louise did most of the talking, afraid that the elderly man might relapse with the effort. 'I love to be out in the open air,' she said. 'Even this close to the centre of town, this place is a lovely haven for wildlife.'

'Yes. I wanted to see if they still have the aviary here.' He coughed and stopped to gather air into his lungs. 'I don't get out much these days. It's been so long, I've forgotten the exact layout of the place.'

She felt a rush of sympathy for him. Had it been so many years since he had a chance to visit the park?

'I remember some years ago they used to have one. I think nowadays it's more of a pets corner for the children—rabbits and guinea pigs and the occasional quail scrabbling about.'

'Ah…' He nodded. 'Things change, don't they?' He looked at her, a gentle, indulgent smile on his face. 'But I can see that you're a girl after my own heart, Louise. May I call you Louise?'

'Of course.'

'Thank you. I'm Joseph. You've been very kind to me and I want to thank you for all that you've done. I feel guilty about this. I'm sure you must be busy and I'm taking up so much of your time.'

'That's all right, and you don't need to feel guilty at all. I'm happy to be here with you. As things stand, I'm able to take a slightly longer lunch break today. But, whatever happens, I won't leave you until you're safely on your way home.'

He patted her hand once more in acceptance of that, and it was as she was returning the gesture that she became aware of a man striding purposefully towards them.

She looked up, casting a thoughtful glance over him as he approached. Like his grandfather, he was well-dressed, wearing a grey suit, though the jacket hung open to reveal a crisply laundered shirt with a pale, faintly striped design. She wondered if he was a businessman of some sort.

He was tall, long-legged, and his demeanour was resolute, the jut of his strong jaw signalling a man who was used to being in charge.

His gaze flicked over her. 'Are you the lady who called me? Louise Bridgford?'

She nodded. 'That's right. I am.'

'Thank you for calling me, and for staying here with my grandfather. I appreciate it.' Then he turned his attention to Joseph, and his matter-of-fact manner changed to one of concern. 'How are you feeling?' he asked, hunkering down, his knees bent so that he could be at eye level with him.

Louise let her glance wander over the beautiful cut of his black hair, noting its springy texture. The hair seemed to reflect the man. It shimmered faintly in the sunlight, with not a strand out of place, and she judged that each fibre was thick and strong.

'I'm fine now. This young lady here, Louise, has been a great help to me.'

James subjected her to another quick scrutiny before turning back to his grandfather. He nodded. 'I'm glad to hear it, but what happened to you? Was it just that you felt short of breath, or did you actually collapse?'

'I just felt a bit peculiar,' Joseph told him. 'I'm feeling much better now.'

James appeared to be giving that some thought. 'The car isn't too far away. I've brought it as far into the park as I could. I'm just wondering if you're going to be able to manage the walk.'

'Yes… I think I can do that, if you just give me another minute or two.'

'Hmm.' James was doubtful. 'Perhaps it would be better if I called for the paramedics. You should probably have someone look you over at the hospital.'

'No. I don't want that.' Joseph's voice was firm. 'I wouldn't like that at all. I'll walk back to the car.' He made to get up and, seeing how the colour immediately drained from him, both James and Louise gently pressured him back down into his seat.

'I think I might have a solution,' Louise murmured, getting to her feet.

James stood up and came alongside her, both of

them moving a short distance from where his grandfather was sitting. 'And what might that be?' he asked.

'I work at the hospital just across the way. I could go over there and borrow a wheelchair. It shouldn't take me more than a few minutes to go and organise that.'

'That seems like a good idea. Would there be any objection to you doing that?'

She shook her head. 'I think they trust me enough to know that I'll bring it back. There's just the question of whether you could sit and wait with your grandfather that long.'

James gave her an odd look. 'I'm not sure that I know what you mean.'

'As far as I understand it,' she said, giving him a direct stare, 'you were with your grandfather when you suddenly went off and started to deal with your phone calls. Do I have that right?'

'Partly.' He frowned. 'We were at the café, and I received a phone call that was quite urgent. The signal wasn't too good, so I left my grandfather enjoying a cup of tea and a bun and went to deal with it outside.'

She guessed that he had been so taken up with dealing with his call that afterwards he had forgotten all about his grandfather. Of course he wasn't going to admit that to her, was he?

'Well, I sincerely hope that isn't going to happen again, because it's very important that you stay with him. You can't be sure that his condition won't worsen—in fact, if I were you, I would be on the alert to call out the emergency services.'

She glanced down at the watch on her wrist. 'I shall have to get a move on. Will you be here when I get back? Can I rely on you?'

He gave her a narrowed stare and she had the impression that he didn't like being questioned that way. He made as if to say something, but then he must have thought better of it because he simply waved a hand in a gesture of acceptance, urging her to go ahead.

'I'll be here,' he said.

Louise set off at a brisk pace and within a few short minutes she was back at the hospital. 'Is it all right if I take one of these wheelchairs?' she asked the senior registrar in charge of the adult A&E unit. 'I'll bring it back in less than half an hour.'

'Go ahead,' the registrar told her. 'Are you okay? Is there a problem?'

'Nothing I can't handle,' she told him. 'Thanks, Taylor.'

When she arrived back at the park, James was pacing across the grass in front of the oak tree. Joseph was sitting where she had left him, and he looked more weary than ever, as though his fighting spirit had gone. She wondered if he was even aware of them being around.

'Has something happened?' she asked.

Perhaps it was more of an accusing stare than a questioning glance that she directed towards James, because he stopped pacing long enough to give her a startled look.

'No, nothing. What did you think might have gone

on? I'm not exactly sure what opinion you have of me, but I do care for my grandfather, very much so.'

She didn't respond, and he tacked on, 'I think he must have some kind of chest infection, and I'll probably have to call the doctor out to him once we get home. The trouble is, he can be quite determined once he's made up his mind about something, and I don't think it would have been worth the stress that would have followed if I had tried to take him to the hospital.'

'Well, I have the wheelchair and a blanket, so we should be able to get him back to your car easily enough now.' She started to walk towards Joseph, adding, 'As to the rest of what you said, I just have a problem with somebody who lets his work take priority over family responsibilities. I can't fathom what could be so important that it can't wait until you're back in the office. No matter what you said, I was actually relieved to come back and find that you were still here.'

James was already starting to help his grandfather into the wheelchair. He settled the blanket around him, his movements gentle and solicitous, but there was a hint of tension in the fixed shape of his mouth.

'Some calls can't be ignored,' he said in a low voice. 'Perhaps you don't have anything of importance going on in your life, or you would have some understanding of that.'

Her green eyes flashed a warning. 'I wouldn't go there if I were you,' she said, her voice ominously quiet.

Joseph stirred and looked from one to the other.

'Have I missed something?' he asked. 'You two are not arguing, are you?'

James laid a hand on his shoulder. 'No, Grandad. Everything's fine.'

'Good, good,' Joseph managed. 'I'm sorry to be so much trouble to everyone.'

'You mustn't think that way,' James said. 'Hold tight, now. I'm just going to wheel you over to the car and we'll get you home where you'll be more comfortable.'

Joseph nodded, and looked up at Louise as she walked beside the chair. 'I've so enjoyed coming out to the park.'

She gave him a smile. 'And you should do it more often when you're feeling better,' she said.

She directed her attention towards James. 'You should remember that people like to get out into the fresh air from time to time, especially the elderly, who might be fed up of being cooped up in their little bungalows, or staring at the walls of their tiny flats day after day.'

She might have expected that James would throw her a terse reply. After all, she was having a quiet dig at him, ramming home the impact of his neglect of his grandfather, but she was surprised to see a faintly amused smile playing over his lips.

She was also startled by how just the hint of a curve to his mouth could affect the way he looked. It dawned on her that he was simply breathtaking, totally masculine in a way that would make any girl's heart begin to flutter. She braced herself, shoring up her defences.

'I'm sure you're right,' he said, his grey glance moving over her in an appraising fashion.

She thought he might enlarge on that statement, but he remained silent after that and it was her turn to be puzzled.

By now, they had reached James's car. It was a sleek silver Mercedes, gleaming in the light of the sun, and she guessed that the inside was every bit as opulent as it appeared on the outside. His dedication to his work had obviously paid off.

What he lacked in family feeling, he obviously made up for in his business acumen.

James helped his grandfather into the car and settled him in his seat. Then he turned to Louise and asked, 'Might I give you a lift anywhere? I could always fold up the wheelchair and put it in the boot.'

She shook her head. 'No, thank you. I have to be getting back to work and it's only five minutes walk away from here.'

She leaned down to take a last look at Joseph. 'You take care,' she told him. 'And make sure that your grandson looks after you properly.'

'I will. Thank you for everything, Louise.'

She stepped away from the car, allowing James to close the passenger door.

'I should add my thanks too,' he said. 'It was good of you to stay with my grandfather and take care of him. We're in your debt.'

'I was glad to help.'

He inclined his head a fraction towards her and then

moved around to the driver's side and slid in behind the wheel. He raised a hand in acknowledgement before starting the engine.

Louise watched as he drove smoothly away out through the park gates, and it was only when she had lost sight of them that she let out a faint sigh. She hoped that Joseph would be all right.

Then she glanced once more at her watch and realised that her lunch break was over. Her shoulders slumped. She hadn't even got around to eating her sandwiches.

CHAPTER TWO

'I WASN'T expecting to find you still here, Louise,' Alice said, coming over to the central desk and putting packages in the box that was to go to the laboratory for testing. 'Don't you have somewhere else to be?'

'Yes, a management meeting.' Louise grimaced before adding her signature to her own set of laboratory forms. 'I just wanted to finish off a few things before I go—tidy up the loose ends, so to speak.'

Alice laughed. 'I'll translate that to mean that you're playing for time and trying to avoid the issue.'

Louise wrinkled her nose. 'I have to admit, I'm not actually looking forward to a confrontation with the executives. This whole business of possible closure has messed everything up and made me feel as though we're in limbo. It's difficult to plan for the future when you don't know if there's going to be one.'

Alice nodded in sympathy. 'I know what you mean. There are staffing problems to contend with, and you were thinking about doing something to brighten the place up a bit, weren't you? I suppose that will have to be put on hold now.' She frowned. 'Actually, I meant to ask you how the interviews for the Senior House Officer went last week, but it slipped my mind when we were talking about the old gentleman you met in the park. You were worried about him, as I recall.'

'Yes, I was. In fact, even now, some days later, I still find myself thinking about him. I only met him for a short time, but he was such a lovely man. I can't help wondering if his grandson is taking proper care of him, but it seemed to me that he must have been more concerned about his business interests than looking after his grandfather's welfare.'

'To be fair, he did come as soon as you called him.'

'Yes, I suppose that's true.' Louise picked up a file from the table and glanced through it. 'As to the interviews, things didn't go all that well, as it happens.' Her mouth made a brief downward turn. 'There weren't any candidates who had sufficient paediatric experience, as it turned out, and those who were well qualified made an excuse and dropped out. I expect they heard about the threat of A&E being closed down and thought better of their applications.'

'That's going to make life difficult for you, isn't it?' Alice was frowning.

'It will be hard on all of us,' Louise murmured. 'We all have to take on the extra workload, and yet there could be months of uncertainty ahead of us. We won't know for some time whether the closure will go ahead, because today's meeting is just the first stage of proceedings. The proposal has to go through the review process, and all the options for change have to be considered by various committees before a final decision can be made.' She pulled a face. 'Though, the way people in charge have been talking, it sounds as though it's pretty much a foregone conclusion. How do you fight a steamroller when it's bearing down on you?'

She studied the file, analysing the notes made by the triage nurse, and then went over to the light box to check the X-ray film that accompanied the notes. 'I think I just about have time to go and look at this next patient,' she told Alice. 'She's a twenty-two-month-old infant who's been vomiting for the last few days, poor thing. After that, I'll be off upstairs.'

She sent a quick smile in Alice's direction. 'It's good to have you working with me here in the A&E unit, Alice. I always feel that I can rely on you. Things seem to run that much more smoothly when you're around.'

Alice's mouth curved. 'I'm glad to be here, although I must say I do like the variety of alternating between the children's ward and A&E.' As an afterthought, she added, 'Though whether the children's ward will survive without A&E is another matter. It seems to me that we're all going to be looking for new jobs.' She made a face. 'It looks as though we're counting on you to defend the territory.'

'I'll do my best.' Louise left her to organise the transfer of samples to the laboratory and went along to the treatment room, where her patient was waiting with her mother. The child was lying on a bed, looking frail, and her mother was sitting beside her, holding the little girl's hand.

'Hello, Mrs Watson,' Louise said in a friendly fashion, going over to the bedside. 'I'm Dr Bridgford. I understand Millie has been unwell for a few days, is that right?'

The child's mother nodded. 'I think she's getting worse. Apart from being sick, she keeps crying, and she just isn't herself. I think she must be in pain.'

'I'll take a look at her.' Louise gently checked the infant over, speaking to her all the while in a soft voice, trying to put her at ease. The little girl was lethargic, though, and her eyes had a sunken appearance. She was fretful and when Louise examined her tummy there appeared to be some tenderness there. 'Does that hurt? I'm sorry, baby. We're all done now.'

She covered the infant with the sheet once more. She wanted to soothe Millie and let her know that she would take care of her, but first they had to find out what was causing the problem.

'There certainly seems to be some tenderness in her tummy now,' she told the mother. 'We've taken blood tests and done a chest X-ray, but we still don't have sufficient information at the moment to be able to make a correct diagnosis. There is some sign that there is pressure at the base of her left lung, but there could be a number of reasons for that.'

'Do you think it's an infection of some sort?'

'I don't think so. She's not particularly feverish, and there are no indications of wheezing to point in that direction, but we'll know more on that score once we get the results back from the lab. In the meantime, I'm going to order some more tests, including an abdominal X-ray so that we can get a better idea of what's going on. She'll be given a barium drink to swallow so that everything will show up on the X-ray as the fluid passes through her intestines. The procedure won't cause her any pain but it will help us to discover if there's anything amiss.'

Mrs Watson still looked anxious and Louise comforted her, saying, 'Don't worry. We'll find out what's causing the trouble.'

They spoke for a little while longer, and then Louise gave Millie an encouraging smile in the hope that it would help to reassure her. There was still no reaction from the little girl. The child was miserable, clearly too ill to respond.

Louise started to write out the test forms for the nurse in attendance.

'I'll leave that with you, Jenny, if I may?' she told the nurse. 'Will you let me know the results when they come through? I'll be in a meeting with management, but you can bleep me.'

Jenny nodded. 'I will.' She was a reliable young woman, with fair hair swept back into a ponytail and blue eyes that missed nothing. Louise knew that she was leaving the child in good hands.

To the mother, Louise added, 'If you have any questions, just ask our nurse here. She'll be able to tell you anything that you want to know.'

'Thank you.'

A moment or two later, Louise was ready to make

her way to the top floor room where management was holding its meeting. She stopped off in the doctors' lounge to pull a brush through her long hair, satisfied that it gleamed with health and was pinned back satisfactorily with a couple of clips. She added a light touch of lipstick to her mouth, and then smoothed down her skirt and checked that her cotton top was neat beneath the light jacket she was wearing. The jacket nipped in at the waist, making the most of her slender form, and she contented herself with making a last adjustment to the collar before she felt confident that she looked all right.

A few minutes later, she tapped on the door of the conference room and took a deep breath to steady herself before walking in.

'Ah, Dr Bridgford, do come in.' The chief executive of the hospital Trust board rose from his seat to greet her. 'I'm so glad that you've managed to find time to come and join us. We do value your input.'

She acknowledged him in a friendly enough manner, although inwardly she absorbed his remarks with a fair degree of cynicism. Since he was the one who had instigated the call for closure, she wasn't about to go overboard with enthusiasm for anything he had to say, was she?

'I think you know most of the people here, don't you?' the chief went on, waving a hand around the room in the direction of the assembled management team.

'I believe so,' she agreed, glancing briefly at the men

and women who were seated around the large rectangular table. Some were other executives from around
the region, but there were a number of people who she
had been working with in this hospital for a few years
now. For the most part they were much like herself,
doctors or managers who were doing the best job they
could, trying to cope in difficult circumstances.

'Please, do come and sit down,' Mr Jeffries urged
her. 'We were just about to go over the options for
change.'

She glanced to where a seat had been left empty for
her and started forward, but as her glance skimmed the
people on either side of that chair she came to an abrupt
halt, the breath snagging in her lungs. There was one
man there who surely didn't belong amongst this collection of medical chiefs.

James Ashleigh flicked a glance over her, his grey
gaze wandering along the length of her shapely legs to
the tips of her fashionably designed shoes, and back
again to rest thoughtfully on the oval of her face. She
faltered momentarily.

Mr Jeffries must have noticed her hesitation because
he said helpfully, 'Ah, of course you won't have met Dr
Ashleigh, will you? He's been working overseas for a
while on secondment, but we are really pleased to have
him back amongst us.'

Louise blinked. So James Ashleigh was a doctor? He
must be a pretty successful one, by all accounts, if he
drove a top of the range Mercedes. Unless, of course,
he wasn't that kind of doctor. Perhaps he had a degree

in economics. That would certainly explain his presence here. Was he one of the wretched money-counters who were intent on eliminating her A&E unit?

She frowned and stared at him once more.

'Dr Bridgford and I have already met.' James Ashleigh returned her gaze with a faintly quizzical expression. Had he guessed what she was thinking?

'Good, good,' Mr Jeffries approved.

Louise inclined her head in acknowledgement and then went and sat down beside James, put out by the way his glance shimmered over her, and out of sorts that he was here at all.

'I hope your grandfather is feeling better by now,' she said in a low tone under the buzz of general conversation in the room.

'His breathing's better than it was,' he answered as the assembly began to settle down. 'His GP prescribed antibiotics, which helped a bit, but my grandfather's heart has been failing for some time now, I'm afraid. He'll never be the man he once was.'

Her mouth flattened. 'I'm sorry to hear it.' She was even more sorry that his grandson couldn't be trusted to take proper care of him. He couldn't possibly be a medical doctor, could he? Where was his sense of responsibility and commitment?

'So, let's get on with the business at hand, shall we?' Mr Jeffries began, calling the meeting to attention. 'The main proposition before us is that we work towards centralising key services at the Royal Forest Hospital. This is part of a rational planning process that we hope will improve the way we serve the region and I'm looking to all of you to help find the best way we can devise our strategy.'

There was a rumble of comment from around the table as people sought to add their views.

'Our most valuable resource is manpower,' one man said, after some general discussion. 'We should see to it that we have the best, most skilled specialists gathered together at the Royal Forest site. That's where the cutting-edge equipment is based—high-performance scanners, new operating suites, and an up-to-the-minute range of telecommunication devices. Specialists can even offer advice over video links without having to travel from one base to another.'

'That won't be a whole lot of use if the departments in outlying hospitals have been closed down, will it?' Louise murmured. She could feel herself getting prickly already.

'We're not talking about taking away necessary resources,' the man answered. 'We're just redistributing them in order to provide a better service.'

Her mouth twisted. 'You mean you're tidying up as part of a cost-cutting exercise.'

Beside her, James Ashleigh stirred. 'Not at all,' he intervened. 'It's more a question of making the best of what we have. Now that we have to comply with directives about junior doctors' working hours, it's becoming even more difficult to maintain full coverage of departments. It makes sense to concentrate them in one centre of excellence.'

Louise gave him a narrow-eyed stare. 'I would have thought the community deserved excellence from all quarters.' Warming to her theme, she added, 'And what will happen to patients who come from outlying regions and don't have a chance to make it to this magnificent centre you're proposing? It's a well-known fact, backed up by research, that people with serious breathing difficulties are less likely to survive a journey to hospital if it's more than six and a half miles away. It's quite likely that patients will die if this plan goes ahead.'

James frowned. 'Do you think you might be in danger of overlooking the part our ambulance personnel have to play in all this? After all, every day they make life-saving interventions while they transport sick people to hospital.'

'Some do, I'll grant you,' she answered in a clipped tone. 'But what happens if you're unfortunate enough to be transported by a technician who isn't allowed to carry out invasive clinical procedures or administer the necessary drugs? There's a high percentage of ambulance personnel who aren't trained to the same extent as paramedics.'

'That's an issue that's being addressed.' His tone softened as though he would appease her in some way. 'You have to take on board the fact that advances in technology are being made all the time, and we need to centralise resources in order to keep pace with what's happening.'

Sparks flared in her green eyes. 'Are you suggesting that I'm out of touch? I can assure you, Dr Ashleigh, that I work with state-of-the-art equipment every day. I suppose you think the community would be better served if it were to be reallocated, in its entirety, to the Royal Forest Hospital along with my patients?'

He made a negligent movement of his hands. 'I didn't say that. I wouldn't like you to feel that this is in any way personal, Dr Bridgford. I'm merely pointing out that we all have to accept that things can't always stay the same, no matter how much we might want them to.'

Louise drew breath, ready to come back at him, but Mr Jeffries cleared his throat and stalled her.

'Of course your opinions will be taken into account, Louise. This is merely a preliminary meeting to discuss the various alternatives. We all know how concerned you are about the effect these changes might have on your department. That's why we need to be particularly careful in how we decide on what options are to be presented to the committee.'

Louise subsided, but inside anger was simmering. She might have known that James Ashleigh would be in favour of destroying what she had built up over these last few years. What did he know about the way she worked? Her patients meant everything to her. They were a huge part of her life, almost like family to her, and she protected the paediatric A&E unit she had shaped as if it sheltered her own little brood. He was all theory and management-speak.

The meeting progressed, and she contented herself with directing a frosty glare in James Ashleigh's direction. He might think that this wasn't personal but, when all was said and done, it wasn't his carefully nurtured project that was being demolished, was it? After that, she made a concentrated effort to push him out of her mind altogether.

Her good intentions only lasted up until they adjourned for a coffee break in an adjoining room. She would have liked to distance herself from him, but he thwarted her by coming to stand next to her in the queue by the coffee machine and engaging her in conversation.

'Can I get you something to eat along with your coffee?' he volunteered. 'I seem to be a little closer to the refreshments than you are. I can offer you biscuits, or there are even sandwiches and pasties, if you'd prefer.'

She shook her head. 'Coffee will be just fine for me, thank you.'

'Do you take it black, or with cream and sugar?'

'Cream and sugar, please.' She accepted the cup he offered her and moved away from the side of the room, looking around for a table where she could sit and mull over what had been said at the meeting. The consensus of opinion among the region's chiefs was still that the paediatric A&E could be wound down, and the objections of the various doctors present had been nudged to one side.

'Do you mind if I join you?'

She looked up to see that James Ashleigh's hand was resting lightly on the chair next to hers. She inclined her head. 'Feel free.'

He sat down, stretching out his long legs underneath the table. The movement was distracting, to say the least. She would have preferred to ignore the fact that he was close by, but he was altogether too masculine a figure and her intentions were doomed from the outset. Her heart began to thump in a chaotic rhythm and her mouth went dry. He was long and lean and totally disturbing to her peace of mind.

As before, at the park, he was dressed in an immaculate, beautifully tailored dark suit, with a crisp mid-blue shirt that looked as though it had come fresh from an exclusive store. His tie was perfectly coordinated, subtle and carefully knotted, as though he was a man who paid a great deal of attention to detail.

She made an attempt to recover herself. 'Has your grandfather been ill for a long time?' she asked.

He nodded. 'Unfortunately, yes. His consultant is doing what he can to ease things for him, by giving him tablets to regulate the heart rhythm, and diuretics to ease his lungs. The trouble is, my grandfather finds it hard to accept his limitations. I dare say that's why he went walkabout last week.'

A small line indented her brow. 'I don't quite follow. He said that you left him to go and make your phone calls. I was under the impression that you didn't go back for him.'

James's mouth made a wry shape. 'I wondered if that was the notion you were left with. No wonder you were a little distant with me.' He stirred his coffee, the action concise and methodical. 'The fact is, I was on call that day, and my Senior House Officer phoned for advice. I stepped outside for a few moments to deal with the situation but, when I returned, my grandfather had disappeared. He does that sometimes. I think he gets a kind of wanderlust and forgets that he isn't able to do what he used to.'

For a moment she was taken aback by this new piece of information, and she wondered distractedly whether she ought perhaps to reassess her opinion of him. He had everything going for him, after all—charisma in bucket-loads and a charm that could melt stone. Maybe she could allow herself to relax a little and get to know him better.

But then she recalled the way he had talked the committee around to his way of thinking just a few minutes earlier and she hardened her heart all over again. Perhaps he had been called away unexpectedly that day but, as a doctor, he should have paid more attention to his grandfather's needs.

'Perhaps you should take him out and about more often. That way he won't feel as though he's housebound and become desperate to escape. I rather had the impression that he feels he's missing out on life sometimes, but I suppose, if you've been away, you won't have realised that.'

She took a sip of her coffee, watching him over the rim of her cup.

He gave her a faint smile. 'I can see that I'm not going to redeem myself in your eyes, whatever I say. I suppose it doesn't help much that we're at opposite sides of the fence when it comes to this business of the hospital.'

'There is that,' she agreed. She frowned, putting down her cup. 'From what you said, I gather that you work here, at the hospital, but you do tend to come across more as management than as someone from the medical staff.'

She had noticed that people tended to listen carefully to what he had to say. They treated him with respect, as though he was someone in authority, someone who had the power to make sweeping changes.

She studied him thoughtfully for a moment or two. 'I've been here at the hospital for a number of years,' she added. 'Even so, I don't recall seeing your name on the list of physicians working at the hospital, but perhaps that's because you've been away.'

He nodded. 'I've been studying different management systems in Europe for the last year. Before that, I was one of the executives at the Royal Forest Hospital. Still am, for that matter, but I tend to divide my time between there and here. I still do hands-on medicine, but to a much lesser degree. I found that I could make more of a difference by being part of the management system.'

Surely he was very young to have reached the pinnacle of his career so soon? She sent him a sceptical look. 'You opted out,' she said.

His mouth twisted. 'I don't see it that way.'

She might have answered him, but her bleeper went off just then and she excused herself to make a call from her mobile phone. 'Hello, Jenny,' she said. 'Do you have some news for me?'

'I do. Millie's results are back from radiology, and the report says that there is a diaphragmatic hernia which has allowed part of the child's intestine to push through to the chest cavity.'

'Oh, dear. No wonder the poor child is suffering. She'll have to go for surgery to have that put right. Put out a call for Mr Simons, will you, and see if he can add her to this afternoon's theatre list. I'll come back right away. I'd better explain things to the mother. In the meantime, we need to make sure Millie's fit to be operated on.'

'I'll do that. Thanks, Louise.'

She cut the call and looked around, to see that James was still there across the table from her. He finished off his coffee and said quietly, 'Problems?'

'A toddler who needs urgent surgery,' she told him. 'I'll have to go back down to paediatric A&E to make sure that everything's in order.'

'You won't be coming back to the meeting?'

'I doubt it,' she said, slanting him a direct glance. 'Some of us have to deal with the sufferings of patients up-front. Fortunately for them, there are still doctors who care enough for their well-being to keep on with the hands-on side of medicine. We leave it to others to move us about like chess pieces on a board.'

She didn't stay to witness his reaction to that, but she could feel his gaze boring into her spine as she walked away from him.

CHAPTER THREE

'IT WAS good to see Millie looking so much better, wasn't it?' Louise made a swift check of the list of patients waiting to be seen and then glanced across to where Jenny was collecting fresh dressings from a cupboard. 'The surgeon discovered a twisting in her intestines as well as the diaphragmatic hernia, so the operation was a little more complicated than we might have expected. I thought it would take longer than a few days for her to recover.'

Jenny smiled. 'I was so pleased when Mrs Watson brought her in. I didn't know whether you would get the chance to see her. I know that you've been busy in the treatment rooms all day.'

'Her mother waited until I was free,' Louise explained, noting down which patients were to be allocated to each of the doctors on duty. 'She said she wanted to thank us for looking after her little girl. It was so lovely to see the child looking well and happy.'

'That's one of the delights of the job, isn't it…seeing the little ones back up on their feet again, ready to cause mayhem.'

Louise chuckled. 'It is, definitely.'

A moment or two later, the phone at the central desk started to ring. It was the line that warned them of incoming patients and Jenny hurried away to answer it, just as James Ashleigh walked into the department.

He was dressed immaculately, as ever, in a grey suit and a crisp pale shirt.

Louise paused briefly in writing up her allocations on the board and half turned towards him, sending him a swift glance before straightening up to face him properly. Why was it that he always managed to make such an impact on her? He had an undeniable presence, a way of grabbing her attention and stopping her in her tracks.

What was he doing here? She braced herself. He was management, and that probably meant trouble.

'I wasn't expecting to see you around here,' she murmured. 'Is there something you wanted?'

He hesitated momentarily, his gaze flicking over her, and from the slightly arrested look in his eyes, it gradually dawned on Louise that her stretch cotton top had shifted a fraction as she had reached up to the board. She quickly smoothed it back into place, ensuring that her midriff was adequately covered and that her pencil-slim skirt was tidy.

He had obviously gathered himself together during that small space of time, because he smiled faintly and there was a glint of humour in the depths of his grey glance. 'Now there's an interesting question,' he said in a husky drawl, his gaze coming to settle on the gentle curve of her hip. 'But, given that we haven't started off our relationship in a particularly good way, I think I'd better forgo the answer that springs to mind.'

Her eyes widened and her knees went weak. Was he actually saying what she thought he was saying? Was he making a pass at her? She felt a surge of heat flow through her entire body as the after-shock of awareness rocked her. The way he looked at her was purely male…discreetly disguised, but full of masculine appreciation, all the same, and she didn't know how she felt about that. After all, he was the enemy. Why was she even contemplating how it might feel to get to know him better?

Covering her confusion, she said shortly, 'I believe we have a patient coming in by ambulance, as well as a waiting room full of children needing to be seen. If you're here to pass the time of day, I'm afraid we're rather busy.'

He inclined his head a fraction. 'I had anticipated that. Until we devise foolproof preventative measures where traffic and accidents are concerned, A&E is always going to be a hectic place.'

He glanced around the central area. 'I must say, this is one of the more cheerful departments I've seen. It's colourful and child-friendly, with all the jungle scenes painted on the walls. I noticed that you have toys in the waiting areas too, and tables set aside for activities.'

'I'm glad that you approve,' she said in a calm manner. 'I was thinking of adding a couple of pictures to the treatment rooms that still look a bit bare… With all the worry about closure, I had put it on hold, but I think I'll go ahead anyway. I don't see why the children should miss out just because the adults are squabbling.'

'I can understand why you would want to do that.' He took another look around the central area, noting the rooms that led off all around. They were glass fronted to allow for easy viewing. There was an uncluttered appearance about the place, and Louise had done her best to make it pleasant for parents who had to wait for news of their sick children, as well as for the youngsters themselves.

'We also have a play leader, to make sure that the little ones are occupied and diverted through what might be a difficult time.' Her gaze narrowed on him. 'You seem to be quite interested in the layout of the place. Is that why you're here? To look around?'

'I'd like to do that. Would it be all right with you?'

She frowned. 'I suppose so.' He obviously had time on his hands if he was able to hang about here, taking note of the surroundings and the general atmosphere. Or was there a hidden agenda to his presence in her department? He was one of the executives, after all, and it went with the territory that they were always on the lookout for any changes that could be made.

Just then, Jenny hurried over to them, saying urgently, 'It looks as though we have an incoming emergency on our hands. He's a three-year-old who's having seizures—apparently he swallowed some of his mum's antihistamine tablets.'

Louise was immediately on the alert. 'Do we know what kind of tablets and how many?'

'Yes. It was dimenhydrinate. The paramedics have taken full note of everything. They're not sure quite how many he took, but they guess it was a substantial amount and it was some time before the mother realised what had happened.'

'Okay—let's get him into the resuscitation room as soon as he arrives. We'll need to hook him up to an ECG monitor and start him on benzodiazepines to control the seizures.'

'I'll go and start making preparations,' Jenny said, hurrying away.

Louise glanced at James. 'I need to head over to the ambulance bay. You'll have to come along with me if you want to talk.'

'That's fine by me.' He walked alongside her as she headed for the main doors.

'Is this visit part and parcel of you wanting to check out the viability of the unit?' She decided that it was better for her to come out with what was on her mind rather than fudge the issue.

'That's a rather harsh way of putting it, don't you think?' His mouth flattened.

Louise gave a faint shrug. 'I don't see any reason not to be blunt,' she murmured. 'That way we both know where we're coming from.'

He acknowledged that with a faint twist to his mouth. 'Let's say that I prefer to see things firsthand. I really need to know what I'm talking about if I'm asked to give an opinion on the various proposals. It's one thing to look at facts and figures that are laid down in reports, and quite another to get a feel for the place and see the way it actually runs.'

'If I were to take that the way it sounds, I might be encouraged to believe there was some hope that you might change your mind about the move to the Royal Forest Hospital.' She made a face. 'On the other hand, I've seen the way these things work at other hospitals, and I suspect that in reality you could be looking into ways you might reorganise the facilities when we're no longer around.'

He laughed. 'You're a cynic through and through, aren't you, Louise?'

Her green eyes flashed. 'Tell me I don't need to be.' It was a definite challenge but, as she expected, he wasn't about to take it up. Perhaps her vehemence startled him, but this department meant everything to her. It was more than a place of work, and she felt an urgent need to defend it and the patients it served. In a way, they were like the family she never had, and she would protect them in any way she could.

She turned away from him as an ambulance siren sounded close by. 'I have to concentrate on the job in hand,' she said. 'If you're going to observe, I hope you'll keep out of the way and let us get on with our work.' It occurred to her that she was perhaps being too dismissive of him, but her priority was with her patients and if he didn't like it that was too bad.

She hurried out to the ambulance bay and observed the small child who was being wheeled in through the main doors of the hospital.

He was in a bad way. He was still having seizures despite the attentions of the paramedics, and his skin was hot and dry. She listened to what the paramedic had to say, and then glanced at the chart he handed her.

'Okay, take him into Resus Two, Andy,' she told him. The young man nodded and did as she suggested. Then he stood back, out of the way, clearly unwilling to leave just then.

Once the child was safely in the room, Louise quickly obtained intravenous access and then administered the drugs that would help stop the seizures.

'Is he going to be all right?' the toddler's mother asked in a shaky voice.

'We're doing everything we can for him,' Louise told her. 'If you'd like to stay by his side and hold his hand and let him know that you're here, I'm sure that will help.'

'Let's get him on oxygen,' she said, glancing at Jenny, 'and we'll do a blood glucose test.'

She worked with the child for several minutes, anxiously watching the monitors and infusing him with various medications as she tried to stabilize his condition.

The Specialist Registrar came to assist. 'The ECG reading is showing a widening QRS complex,' he told her.

She acknowledged him, saying, 'Okay, Tim, we'll start bicarbonate therapy and see if that will settle things down.' Louise glanced anxiously at the monitors once more. 'You had better notify the intensive care unit,' she told Jenny. 'He'll need to be admitted. In the meantime, I'll put in a nasogastric tube so that we can give him activated charcoal and then, as soon as we're able, we'll do a gastric lavage.'

Louise stayed with the child until she had done everything that was possible for him.

'What's going to happen to him?' the boy's mother asked. 'Matthew's so little and he looks dreadfully ill. I just never realised it could get this bad.'

She was naturally distressed, and Louise wished that she could reassure her in some way. 'We'll keep him in our observation bay until ICU can find a bed for him,' Louise told her. 'We've washed out his stomach in case there was any antihistamine still in there, and we're doing what we can to minimise the effects of any of the drug that's in his system. Other than that, it's too soon to tell how things will turn out. We'll know better in a few hours if we've managed to counteract the worst consequences.'

The paramedic was still waiting to see if there were any results. He was a fair-haired young man in his thirties, and Louise knew that he was dedicated to his job.

He was frowning, and Louise went over and spoke to him as she left the child in Jenny's care. She didn't want to leave him at all, but there were other patients who needed her, and all she could do for him now was to wait. 'I'm sorry there isn't any better news for you, Andy,' she told him. 'I suppose you have to get back to work now, don't you?'

Andy nodded. 'I stayed as long as I could.'

'I'll let you know as soon as there is any change,' she promised. 'It's heartbreaking, isn't it, seeing a child in that situation.' She gave a soft sigh. 'He looks so tiny and vulnerable.'

Andy's expression was bleak. 'All I know is that he's in the best hands, with you looking after him. I expect I'll see you later on, Louise.' He lightly touched her arm in a gesture of support before he made his way back to the ambulance bay.

Louise started back towards the central desk and saw that James Ashleigh was waiting for her, his gaze following the paramedic as he left the reception area.

His gaze moved over her and she tried not to let his careful scrutiny throw her. He noticed too much, and it threw her to know that he, of all people, could unsettle her with a mere glance.

'You seem to get on very well with everyone around here,' he commented.

'I find it helps to have a good working atmosphere,' she said lightly. 'We're with each other for many hours in the day and sometimes through the night, and it makes for a much better outcome if everyone gets on well together. That way we work as a team.'

She glanced at him. 'How do you run your department? I take it that you do have a department to oversee, now that you're back in the UK, or are you spending all your time adding up figures and moving papers about?'

He laughed. 'You have a way with words, don't

you?' Sobering, he said, 'It's true that I do oversee a department, but I only actually take a couple of morning clinics and do a ward round in the middle of the week. The rest of the time I'm involved with management duties.'

'Such as you are this afternoon?' She let the statement hang in the air. 'I don't see how you can possibly advise your committee on whether my unit is a success or whether it should suffer the axe, when you've been out of touch with the cut and thrust of hands-on medicine for such a long time. I don't see that a couple of mornings here and there give you much of an edge on the rest of us. But then, that's what you management people are all about, isn't it? You don't see the day-to-day work that goes on. You see costing and services, and a series of numbers to be crunched and targets to be achieved.'

'Some of us have to look at the workings of the hospital from an overall viewpoint, and make decisions about the structure of things. Reorganisation could be the answer to the problems in this region. It isn't a cost-cutting exercise, as you called it, but resources are not infinite.'

She scowled. 'And if one little paediatric A&E unit folds as a result, that's fine, isn't it? Who's going to count the cost of one little boy who swallowed his mother's tablets and might have to travel through rush-hour traffic to get to the Royal Forest Hospital? I don't know whether we've managed to reverse the damage that was done to him, but I do know that he probably wouldn't have stood any chance of making it if he'd been forced to travel to the Royal Forest.'

'You can't say that for certain. Who's to say that the local GP might not have been around to intervene where necessary?'

'I might have known you'd find a way to wriggle around the situation. That's the whole trouble, isn't it? All your ideas are pure theory. You spout all this so-called wisdom, while I have to cope with the day-to-day problems of holding together an overstretched department. You should be pouring resources into it, not closing us down. We need more staff here, but your proposals have put paid to that, haven't they? Who's going to come here and risk being out of a job in a few months' time?'

'Whoa there, steady on.' He put up his hands, palms flat in front of him, as though to stop the onslaught. 'Perhaps it isn't as bad as you think.' He lowered his hands and moved closer to her so that she was disturbingly aware of his long, lean body and the way that he moved, with a suppleness that spoke of lithe energy and keen vitality. 'There's nothing to stop me from coming and working here, is there—for a few months, at any rate?'

He said it in such a casual manner that it took a moment or two for it to sink in. She stared at him. 'I'm not sure that I heard that right. Did I just hear you offer to come and work in my department?'

'Well, I know that you're looking for a Senior House Officer, and I may be a touch overqualified for that, but

I can spare a couple of mornings and maybe a couple of afternoons a week in order to lend a hand. I'm sure we could work something out between us.'

She blinked, and struggling to take in what he was saying. 'I'm actually looking for someone who has paediatric experience,' she managed after a while. 'That's on top of being able to cope with accident and emergency. From what I've heard, you're working in the renal unit, so I'm not quite sure whether you would be the right candidate for the job.'

Even to her own ears it sounded shocking that she should be taking one of the executives to task about his qualifications. Why was it that she felt the need to constantly have a go at this man? It wasn't enough to argue that he was threatening her position here, or even that he didn't take proper care of his grandfather. It was something more than that.

On a basic, primitive level, she felt that she needed to defend herself against him, although she couldn't put into words exactly what it was that she feared. It was enough to put her into attack mode.

'By all means check my credentials,' he said and, to be fair to him, he didn't look at all put out by her misgivings. 'I think you'll find that I have enough experience in both departments to fulfil the criteria. As to my reasons for doing it, let's just say that I can see that you're understaffed, and I'm in a position where I've been away for a while and I haven't yet eased back into my full-time role. I'm in the fortunate position of being able to pick and choose what I want to do.'

'You're highly fortunate, I would say.' Louise recovered her equilibrium and found that she was more than a little sceptical of his motives. He made it sound as though he was doing her a favour, but she had her doubts about that. 'I expect that working in the department will make life far easier for you when it comes to writing up your report, won't it? You'll have all the information you need at your fingertips.'

'Are you afraid to accept my offer?' Again, there was that faint hint of amusement that played around his mouth. It was unsettling, as though he could read her like a book, whereas Louise would be hard put to say what it was that was bothering her.

If his plan was to work with her in order to check up on the day-to-day running of the unit, then she was pretty certain that she could deal with that well enough. She suspected her unease was caused by something entirely different, and it was enough to make her hesitate.

How would she cope with having him in close proximity on a regular basis? He exuded masculinity without even trying, and just knowing that he was around seemed to throw her nervous system into chaos.

'I would have to look into the possibilities,' she told him, playing for time.

He nodded. 'That's okay. I know this must have come as a bit of a shock to you. But I'm sure you'll see the sense in it when you've had time to think things through.' He let his glance run over her, causing a wave of heat to ripple through her veins. 'Perhaps I could take you out to lunch and we could talk things over.'

'Um…' She struggled to compose herself. 'I don't think so, thanks all the same. I have to attend a couple of meetings this afternoon… I suggest we do that some other time.'

Some time never, she told herself. Sitting down to lunch with him seemed like altogether too intimate an occasion. He even made it sound as though it would be something special, the way his voice softened and his eyes took on a warm glimmer. It would be like going to dinner with a wolf and, with him being the way he was, it gave her more the feeling that she was being stalked by the leader of the pack.

'As you please,' he said. 'Perhaps you'll let me know what you decide regarding the offer to join your team.'

'I will.' She realised that her lungs were tight with suppressed air, and now she pulled in a deep breath to lighten her load. 'I'm on the late shift tomorrow, but I could let you know the day after, if that would be all right with you?'

'That's fine by me,' he murmured. 'Reception has my number.' He smiled. He wasn't at all fazed by her reticence, and why should he be? He was the one who was in command, and he knew it.

As for Louise, her nerves were shot to pieces.

CHAPTER FOUR

LOUISE wound down the window of her car, allowing the warm summer breeze to caress her cheeks. It was a good feeling, being able to breathe in the fresh air, and with the gentle heat settling around her limbs she began to relax a little as she drove along the country lanes. The view of the vineyards that graced the southern slopes of the Wye Valley was a treat in itself.

Here and there, she caught glimpses of fruitful orchards, where the trees were beginning to develop the crop of apples that would later be turned into the cider that would eventually be sipped in the local inns.

The Wye Valley was a good place to live and work, and she ought to be thankful that she was able to enjoy it. If it wasn't for the problems that crowded in on her, life might be good. As it was, she didn't seem to have any choice but to make the best of things, and go on as though her prized A&E unit would be safe for the future.

With that thought in mind, she turned the car purposefully towards the town, heading for the art gallery.

Would the pictures she had admired so much still be available there? They would do so much to cheer up her young patients as they waited to have their injuries tended.

'Yes, I still have them,' the young woman at the art gallery told her. 'I could see how interested you were in them, so I put them to one side for a while, just in case you came back.'

She was a pretty dark-haired girl, with long slender fingers and nails that were beautifully manicured, and she had such a good knowledge of paintings that Louise wondered if she was an artist herself.

'I do paint the occasional landscape,' she answered with a smile when Louise gently enquired.

'Gemma's very talented,' a shaky voice put in from across the room. 'She's very modest about her work, but she could stand amongst the best.'

Louise turned to face the elderly gentleman who had spoken. 'Joseph!' she said in pleased surprise, seeing James's grandfather seated by a table in the corner. 'It's good to see you again. What are you doing here? Are you shopping for artwork?' He looked even more frail than before, and she couldn't help thinking that he ought to be at home, resting. Perhaps he had been overcome by fatigue and needed to sit down for a while.

'I just wanted to spend some time out of the house,' Joseph explained. He nodded, as though confirming that to himself, and then his eyes drooped slightly as though he was about to fall into a doze.

Louise turned back to Gemma. 'We met the other

day at the park, when he was feeling unwell. Has the same thing happened again? Is that why he's here—because he needed to rest for a while?'

'My grandfather is just visiting,' Gemma said, looking across the room to the old man.

'Joseph is your grandfather?' Louise echoed.

'Yes, and I love him dearly. He's been more like a father to me.' Gemma's grey eyes were troubled as she turned back to Louise. 'So you must be the doctor he was telling me about.' She smiled in acknowledgement, and then, in an undertone, she added, 'Unfortunately, he's taken to wandering about these last few weeks, and my brother thought he would be better off sitting here with me for an hour or so. That way, I can keep an eye on him. He's not at all well, but he loves to look at the work on display, and talk to some of the artists who come in from time to time.'

So this was James's sister? Louise looked at her more closely, to see if there was any resemblance she could discover... Possibly the angular cheekbones and the eyes that were an unusual mix of grey-blue were the tell-tale features. 'I can imagine he would like to do that. I expect he's a lively old soul usually, isn't he?'

Gemma nodded. 'Usually, but of late he's becoming more and more fragile. I have to confess that I'm worried about him. There seems to be quite a lot of fluid in his chest and he gets very short of breath, and runs out of energy quite fast. James says it's because his heart is failing.'

Louise nodded. 'It must be difficult for you, not

knowing how you can help him if his medication isn't doing the trick. He isn't at all overweight and I expect he already watches his diet and cuts out salt as much as possible. All you can really do is to be here for him and make sure that he isn't in any pain.' She looked fondly at the old man. 'Is he staying with you all day?'

'No.' Gemma kept her voice low. 'At least, he wasn't meant to be staying. My brother was supposed to come and fetch him some time ago, but he's swamped with work and rang to say that he couldn't make it. I must say, I'm more than a little concerned about him just now. He's been quite poorly this morning. It's so sad to see. He used to be so energetic and full of life, but now he seems to be failing fast.'

'I'm sorry.' Louise frowned. What was James thinking of, letting his grandfather down? Fair enough, he was a busy man, but his family ought to come first and if he had promised to come and fetch him, he should be here, shouldn't he? How was it that he was able to offer to come and work with her when he couldn't spare the time to be with his grandfather?

'Anyway, enough of my troubles.' Gemma put on a bright smile. 'You say you'd like to buy these paintings?'

'I would.' Louise looked down at the oil paintings that Gemma had propped up on the counter. 'They're so cheerful and child-friendly, with the bright scenes of children playing. I love the way the beach looks golden and inviting in that one, and how the puppy peeps through the shrubbery in this one.' She was smiling as two small girls came running into the room and came to peer at the landscapes.

'I like the one with the puppy best of all.' The older child who spoke up was the image of Gemma. Her dark hair was silky and swung from side to side as she turned her head. 'He makes me want to stroke him.'

'Me, too. He's adorable, isn't he?' Louise looked from one child to the other and guessed that they were sisters; they had similar features.

'Are these your children?' she asked, glancing at Gemma.

'Yes, they are. Nicola and Anne-Marie.' Gemma indicated each of them in turn. 'Nicola's five years old, and Anne-Marie is six, going on seven.' She winced. 'They have to spend time with me here during the school's summer holidays. It isn't an ideal situation, but at least there's a patch of garden out back where they can play.'

'That's something anyway, and it means that they can be with you while you're working.'

Did that mean that Gemma had no parents or in-laws she could call on to babysit for her from time to time? That was a sad situation, but it was one that Louise could identify with, since she had lost her own parents at a young age and could barely remember them. As for James, he had never mentioned any family, other than his grandfather, but then the question had never arisen, had it?

'So,' Gemma murmured, 'where would you like me to deliver these paintings, or will you be taking them away with you?'

'They're for the hospital, for the children's A&E unit. I'll take them with me. Would it be all right if I pay for them by card?'

'Of course. Perhaps you could give me your home address, for my ledger? There is an insurance cover on them that will last for six months. I'll transfer it to your name.'

'Thanks.' Louise began to write in the ledger that Gemma put before her. 'I live at Watermead House in Brooklea village.'

Gemma's head lifted. 'I think I've heard that name…'

'What's that? What did you say?' Joseph appeared to have woken up with a start. He blinked, gathering himself together.

'We were talking about Watermead House, Grandad,' Gemma told him. 'It's where Louise lives.'

'Watermead… That's a seventeenth century house, isn't it?'

'Yes, it is.' Louise glanced at him, noticing that he was frowning, as though he was trying to jog his memory. The little girls went over to him to give him a hug and he put an arm around each of them. Louise could see that there was a lot of affection between them.

'I haven't lived in the house for all that long,' she added. 'Just around a year, I would think. It took me quite some time to decide on where I was going to stay, but there was a certain appeal to the property that made me want to buy it.'

Joseph nodded. 'It's a listed building, isn't it, one

that the local authority wants to preserve. I think I have a picture of it somewhere.'

Louise lifted a delicately arched brow. 'You do?'

He nodded. 'One of my ancestors had a keen interest in all the old buildings in the area—Brooklea is made up of a number of quaint cottages and the like, isn't it? He built up quite a collection of items to do with local history. Anyway, he bought sketches and paintings of the ones he was particularly fond of. I'm sure I have a painting of your property around the house somewhere.' He coughed a little and Louise could hear the wheezing sound his chest made. 'You'll have to let me show it to you.'

'Thank you, I'd like that,' Louise murmured. 'I'm surprised anyone would have taken the trouble to make a painting of it—it's just a small place and nothing spectacular, although I suppose there's an appealing old world character about it.' She had managed to pick it up at a reasonable price, given that it needed work doing on it to restore it to its former glory.

'That's it, I think. It blends in so beautifully with the surroundings.' The old gentleman looked weary, and she wondered if he was going to have to stay here all day until Gemma was able to close up shop and take him home. He looked as though he ought to be in bed, propped up with lots of pillows, instead of sitting in an upholstered chair in his granddaughter's art gallery.

Just then, though, the main door opened and James walked purposefully into the room. He was tall, loose limbed and energetic, and looked as though he was ready for action. Louise gathered herself up, compelled by the sheer magnetism of the man to follow his every movement, but conscious, at the same time, that she needed to shore up her defences.

Gemma smiled at him. 'I'm glad you managed to get here,' she said softly. 'Grandad's not feeling at all well.'

'I came as soon as I could,' James acknowledged, glancing to where his grandfather was sitting, and then letting his gaze drift over Louise. 'I'll give him one of the ACE inhibitors his GP prescribed. That should help reduce the strain on his heart and help him to feel better.'

'Good. I'll go and fetch a glass of water so that he can swallow it down. And then I'll perhaps be able to concentrate on wrapping up these pictures.' Gemma went over to an annexed room to fetch the drink.

James nodded, then looked properly at Louise, sending a smile in her direction. 'I hadn't expected to see you here.' Then he glanced at the paintings on the counter and inclined his head as though all had become clear. 'I expect those are intended for the hospital, aren't they? You mentioned that you wanted to brighten up a couple of the treatment rooms.'

'Well, someone has to think about the patients,' she said. She delivered the words with a faintly caustic glance in his direction. She would not let him get to her. It was difficult enough getting used to the idea that he had the power to bring down the axe on her department, but the fact that he had let his grandfather down again was bothering her.

For a moment, he looked as though he was taken aback by her barbed comment, but just then his two young nieces claimed his attention, clamouring to be hugged, and he responded by lifting each one up in turn, swinging them around. He laughed as they squealed in delight.

Then, steadying Nicola down on the floor once more, he went over to his grandfather. 'I'm sorry to hear that you're not feeling too good,' he said. 'Shall we get you home, then? I expect you could do with a bit of a snooze and the daily paper to keep you company.'

'Everyone fusses too much,' Joseph muttered. 'I keep telling all of you, I'll be fine.'

'Of course you will. It's just that we don't want you to overdo things.' He studied his grandfather's face. 'Are you ready for me to take you out to the car?'

'No, no, not yet. I want to ask Louise if she's going to come with us. I want her to see the picture.' He made a shaky movement with his hand, as though to move his grandson to one side so that he could see her better.

'The picture?' James was puzzled.

'Watermead House. I have a watercolour of it some-where…or it might be a sketch.' The old man frowned, trying to get his breath.

James looked in Louise's direction, throwing her a questioning glance.

'It's where I live,' she said. 'It really isn't necessary for your grandfather to put himself out. I don't mean to disturb him. I don't want to trouble him in any way. I can see that he's very tired.'

'I thought she might like to have it,' Joseph said, looking up at James as though he expected him to take over and deal with the situation.

'Oh, but I can't let you do that,' Louise protested, realising his intent. 'I wouldn't dream of taking your picture from you.'

'I've no need for it. I have so many.' Joseph's voice became firm, and Louise caught a glimpse of the man he must once have been, a man with all the power and authority that now, in turn, James possessed. He was used to having his own way.

'Do you have time to come with us?' James asked, giving her a direct look. 'Only I think he will just become more agitated if we go against him on this. It's such a small thing, and I don't like to see him going into a decline if it can be avoided.'

Louise couldn't let that pass. She said in a stiff, low tone that only James could hear, 'If that's the case, then perhaps you should have come and taken him home some time ago, instead of claiming to be too busy. How do you expect to come and work with me if you can't even take care of your own grandfather?'

He gave her a startled look. 'I don't know what information you have, but my brother, Robert, was supposed to be coming to fetch him. I only came because Gemma called me and said that Robert couldn't make it. As it is, I've had to come away from a meeting in order to pick him up.'

'Oh, I see.' She was instantly deflated as the breath left her lungs and she felt a tide of warm colour flood into her cheeks. She had done it again, hadn't she? 'I didn't realise that you had a brother. I'm sorry. I can see that I had everything wrong again.'

James's grey gaze captured hers, not allowing her to look away as she would have liked. 'I dare say you could redeem yourself by coming back with us to the house,' he remarked, sliding an arm around her shoulders. 'You're not on duty until mid-afternoon, are you? I could bring you back, so that you'll be able to collect your car.'

Louise tried to ignore the way he was folding her to him. It was altogether too distracting. She thought about what he'd said and then slowly nodded. What choice did she have? 'As long as I'm back in time for my shift.'

'I have to be back at work too.' His expression wryly amused, he let her go. He knew full well that he had won that one all too easily. 'There should be enough time for us to collect the picture and have a bite of lunch.'

'All right.' She was subdued and throughout the process of installing Joseph comfortably in the Mercedes she remained quiet. Gemma and the girls came outside to see them off and Louise waved and gave them all a brief smile.

She was seated in the front of the car, next to James, as he drove them away, and after a while the silence began to get to her. 'I don't think you mentioned your brother Robert before this,' she said.

'No, perhaps not. He normally looks after our grandfather, because they live together up at the house. Mostly, during the day, Robert has to work on running the farm, but he manages to keep an eye on Grandad.'

'Gemma said that he was overwhelmed with work today. Is something out of the ordinary going on?'

'They're harvesting some of the crops, and I gather that one of the animals has fallen sick. He had to call the vet to come and take a look.'

'Oh, I see.' She was still uncomfortable at the depth of her misunderstanding, and James wasn't giving her any indication as to whether he had forgiven her or not. Glancing around, she saw that in the back of the car Joseph was sleeping peacefully.

'It must be difficult for you,' she murmured, 'having to take care of your grandfather, and coping with your own workload. How did you manage when you were away in Europe?'

'I'm afraid the burden fell on my brother and on Gemma. I came home every now and again and took over for a while so that they could have a break, and of course they were always in touch with me in case there were any problems. You're right, though, it hasn't been easy for any of us.'

He sent her a sideways glance before turning his attention back to the road ahead. 'I dare say your job isn't easy, either. I thought you handled the situation with young Matthew very well yesterday. It must have been very worrying for you, knowing how badly he had overdosed, and especially with the mother looking on. It's always difficult to explain to a parent what's happening, and when you're not able to reassure them over the outcome it's distressing all round.'

'That's true. I suppose, after a while, you get used to it, though it doesn't make it any easier to cope when things go wrong.'

'How is the boy, do you know?'

'There hasn't been much change, so far. I spoke to Jenny over the phone this morning and she said he was still very poorly.'

'I'm sorry.'

'So am I. I managed to get him into intensive care yesterday, before I left the hospital. I went to take a look at him, and he was just lying there, not moving, not responsive, and it was heartbreaking.'

'Paediatrics can be a difficult specialty. What is it that makes you go on doing the job, do you know?' He shot her a quick glance before turning the car on to a country lane.

'I'm not sure,' she admitted. 'I often ask myself the same question, but perhaps it comes down to the fact that I look on them like my own children…my own family, really. I never had any brothers or sisters, and I don't remember much about my parents, so the children in my A&E are all very special to me.'

He sent her an oblique glance. 'So what happened to you as a child? Who took care of you?'

She frowned. 'My parents were lost in a tragic accident when we were on holiday and a bus overturned on a mountain pass. I escaped injury, but there were no relatives to take care of me, and so when I was brought back to England I was sent to a children's home.'

A line etched itself into her brow. 'After that, I went to live in various foster homes. Nothing really worked out very well, because there were unexpected problems within the foster families—nothing to do with anything I had done—but it meant that I was moved around quite a bit until I was old enough to fend for myself. It was unsettling.'

His brows met in a dark line. 'It must have been.' He turned the car on to a wide road that led towards huge iron gates. 'You seem to be pretty well adjusted these days, though, so I imagine you must have managed to turn things around for yourself.'

She nodded. 'I think the turning point was when I realised that I wanted to study medicine. Then, when I specialised and started working with children I felt as though I had finally found where I belonged.'

James smiled. 'It's good when that happens.' He stopped the car and pushed open the door on the driver's side, getting ready to step out.

'Are we here?' Louise looked around. She could see a house, set apart among trees, on the other side of the gates. It looked like a lodge on the edge of a large country estate. 'Is this where your grandfather lives…in the lodge?' she asked, waving a hand in the direction of the house. She made as if to get out of the car.

'No, we have a little further to go. Sit tight. I just need to open the gates to the estate.'

'Oh, I see.' She frowned. 'I expect there are a number

of farm cottages dotted around, are there? There must be several farm workers if the land covers a large area.'

'Yes,' he said. 'There are about half a dozen, along with a converted barn and a stable block that has been turned into accommodation.'

Louise settled back into her seat and watched as he unlocked the heavy wrought iron gates. It made sense that his brother would live deeper into the estate, closer to the land he was farming.

Then James came back to the car and drove through the open gates, halting the vehicle once more on a wide driveway while he went to close them again. Ahead, the view was obscured by an avenue of trees that followed the curve of the road.

'I expect your brother has his work cut out for him,' Louise said when they were on the move once more. 'From the look of things, this is a huge estate. I imagine the farm workers are tenants on the land…though I've always wondered what happens to the workers once they leave the job. They don't always have secure tenancy, do they? Does your brother worry about that?'

James was silent for a moment and she wondered if she had overstepped the mark with her questions. 'I'm sorry,' she said. 'It's none of my business; I shouldn't have asked.'

'No, that's all right.' James seemed to be amused by her remark, and Louise couldn't imagine what she had said that would make him smile. 'The question hasn't actually arisen, but I think we could say that Robert is pretty sure of having a home for life,' he murmured.

Louise was so busy watching his expression, that it came as something of a shock when he drew the car to a halt in front of a grand country mansion. It must have dated from around the seventeenth century but, unlike her own house, this was an extremely large property. Her eyes widened.

It was beautiful in its simplicity. Built out of stone, it had three gabled elevations to the front, forming an E shape, and the roof was covered with reddish-brown clay tiles, which added warmth to the whole building. The windows were made up of small rectangular panes of leaded glass, reaching upwards almost to roof level, and the lower windows were set in casements that were surrounded by tall decorative arches formed out of stone.

In front of the whole edifice was a sweeping lawn, bordered by mature trees and shrubs, and all about were flower borders, bright with the colours of lavender, blue and pink.

A small gasp escaped her. 'This is beautiful,' she said, her voice awestruck. 'But why have we stopped here? Do you have to check in at the main house?'

'No.' His gaze meshed with hers. 'This is where we live.'

She stared at him. 'This is your house? I don't understand…'

'The Manor House has been our home for generations, ever since it was first built.'

She blinked, still having difficulty grasping what he was saying. The Manor House was his home? How could that be?

CHAPTER FIVE

LOUISE shook her head. 'I don't think I follow any of this. You said that your brother worked on a farm. I was expecting to find that he lived in a farmhouse.'

James's mouth made an odd shape. 'Perhaps that was the wrong way of putting it. The estate is made up of the house and the land all around. Our income comes mostly from the farmland and the produce that we sell in the farm shops, and my brother oversees all that. Then there's a small amount of income from the tenants who live on the estate, but mostly that's put aside for upkeep of the buildings. My grandfather prefers to keep control of the property side of things.'

Perhaps he had heard himself mentioned in their conversation because, in the back of the car, Joseph stirred. 'What's happening?' he asked. 'Are we home?'

Louise's mouth had dropped open, but now she clamped it firmly shut. When Joseph had talked about wanting to get out and about, she had imagined him sitting in a little house or flat somewhere, staring at the four walls. Not once had it occurred to her that he was surrounded by this vast estate.

'We're here, Grandad. I'll come around and help you out.'

James glanced briefly at Louise. She was still overcome by shock and simply stared ahead. 'Why didn't you tell me, before this?' she asked.

'I thought you knew,' he said simply. 'Most people know about Ashleigh Manor. Though I suppose if you're not originally from around here, it might have passed you by. There's been a Lord Ashleigh in residence at the Manor for centuries.'

Lord Ashleigh? For a moment or two, Louise felt as though her head was spinning. A feeling of faintness washed over her, as though her mind was refusing to take any of this in.

By now, James was helping his grandfather from the car. The old gentleman was unsteady on his feet and that was enough to bring Louise to her senses and make her scramble out of her seat.

'Let me give you a hand,' she murmured, going to assist by supporting Joseph on one side as they climbed the steps that led to the main door.

'Thank you, my dear,' Joseph managed. 'You're like a breath of fresh air that has come into our lives.'

Louise was at a loss as to how to answer that. 'I'm glad you think so,' she said.

'Where would you like to go, Grandad?' James asked when they were inside the house. 'Do you want me to help you up to bed, or would you like to sit in the drawing room for a while?'

'No, no. It's such a lovely day. We'll sit out in the garden.'

'As you like. I'll ask Catherine to bring us some cold drinks out there.'

Louise wondered who Catherine might be. Was she the one who was responsible for the elegant display of flowers that graced the table in the great hall?

They were beautiful, as was everything in this lovely place. Exposed oak timbers arched across the ceiling, burnished to a hue that was golden in colour, and on one side there was a wonderful mezzanine floor, edged with a carved wooden balustrade, overlooking the hall.

'That was the minstrel gallery,' James told her, following the direction of her gaze. 'In years gone by they would hold celebrations in here, and the musicians would sit up there and entertain the guests. Of course, there would be a fire burning in the grate then, to make things more cheerful.' He waved a hand towards the huge carved fireplace that was situated at the far end of the room.

Louise could hardly take it all in. The walls were hung with bright tapestries that enlivened the room with their patterns woven with thread of red and gold. Beneath her, the floor was laid with oak timbers, polished to a sheen that lent warmth to the whole area.

'I'll give you a quick tour later on, if you like,' James offered. 'For the moment, though, I think it would be best if I get my grandfather settled down outside. Catherine will bring us some lunch and, while she is preparing that, I'll go and see if I can hunt out the picture of Watermead House. I'm not quite sure where to begin to look for it. My great-great-grandfather had so many of these things that we've tended to put them away in various places. There aren't enough walls to accommodate his collection.'

'Please don't trouble yourself,' Louise said, as they went out into the lush garden. She helped to settle Joseph in a comfortable lounger chair under the shade of a sprawling cherry tree and glanced at the old man, who had closed his eyes wearily and appeared to be falling into a slumber once more. 'I really feel bad about him offering it to me. I just happened to mention that that's where I'm living. It's a lovely old seventeenth century house and I feel privileged enough to be there. I really don't want to rob you of your picture.'

Joseph's eyes opened. 'I want you to have it,' he said in a wheezy voice. He patted her hand. 'Sit down and keep me company.' He looked at James. 'It might be locked away somewhere in the old chapel. Have a look in there for it.'

James nodded, and then glanced briefly at Louise. 'I hope you don't mind if I leave you alone for minute or two. Catherine will be out in a while with some food. It'll probably be cold cuts of meat and salad, but she always puts on a good spread. I hope you're hungry.'

'That's okay. Thank you.' Louise's whole perception of him and his family had been turned on its head in a matter of minutes, and she wasn't at all sure that she could manage a morsel, but she supposed no one would notice if she was to hold back from eating.

'This part of the garden is glorious,' she said, turning to Joseph as James left them. They were seated by a white wrought iron table, and all around there were flower borders filled with glorious country garden flowers—tall hollyhocks, lupins, foxgloves and, at a lower level, bright purple phlox.

'Yes, it is. I like to sit out here of an afternoon,' Joseph agreed. 'I like the scent of the honeysuckle.'

'It's very fragrant and it's easy to see why you would enjoy being out here, especially on a day like this.'

He nodded. 'I'm glad you were able to come here with us today. James told me that you are working at the same hospital, and I was hoping that I would see you again.'

He stopped speaking as a middle-aged woman came across the lawn towards them. She was carrying a tray, set out with jugs of iced juice of different flavours and tall glasses, along with a selection of hors d'oeuvres.

'These are just to keep you going until I bring out the main course,' the woman said.

'Thank you, Catherine.' Joseph smiled at the woman, who returned his gaze with a curve of her mouth. 'This is Louise, the doctor who's working with James. Louise, this is our housekeeper, Catherine. She's a treasure. We really couldn't manage without her.'

He indicated Louise, by his side, and she greeted the housekeeper in return. 'Hello, Catherine. Thanks for this. It looks delicious.'

'You're very welcome.' Catherine had a friendly face, with soft blue eyes and feathery brown hair that framed her face. 'I heard how you went to help Joseph the other day. We appreciate what you did, very much.' She glanced at the table. 'I'll bring the food out in a moment.'

By now, James had come out of the house and was striding across the lawn towards them. He was holding a framed picture, about eighteen inches wide, and as he approached he showed it to Louise.

'It's in really good condition, considering that it was painted over a century ago,' he said. 'Do you think the house has changed very much from the outside since this was done?'

Louise looked down at the watercolour he showed her. 'No,' she told him. 'It's pretty much the same, except that it looks as though the roof has been tiled over since that time. Of course, you can't see round the back of the house from this painting, but a kitchen was built onto the house around a hundred years ago, so the local historians tell me.' She glanced up at him. 'This is a wonderful picture.'

'The picture is yours to keep,' Joseph said. 'I'm glad that you like it.'

Louise was about to object, but a look from James stilled her. 'Please take it,' he said. 'My grandfather wants you to have it.'

Louise could see from the set of his jaw and from the look of contentment on Joseph's face that she was fighting a losing battle. 'Thank you,' she said. 'It's lovely, and I'm very grateful to you. I shall give it pride of place in my living room.'

'Good. Artwork like that takes us back in time, but it takes us forward as well, into the future.' Joseph made an odd little smile and then sat forward in his seat. 'Ah, here comes lunch.'

Louise wasn't at all sure what he'd meant by that remark about the future. Perhaps he'd simply meant that paintings could show the passage of time.

Catherine had done them proud with a delicious honey roast ham, part of which was already carved for them, and that was accompanied by roast chicken and a platter of nibbles, including chicken goujons and stuffed tomatoes. Added to these, there was a variety of cheeses, a dish of salad, herb mayonnaise dips, a selection of relishes and a basket of different types of bread.

'Will you try some crab cakes?' James asked, handing her a plate and reaching out to serve her with an assortment of food.

'Thank you.' Louise suddenly discovered that she had an appetite after all. She might well be in the wolf's lair, but at the moment he was a fairly amenable wolf, and even though that might be because his grandfather was present, she felt relaxed enough to let her guard down a little.

She tasted the food and discovered that it was every bit as mouth-watering as it appeared. 'This is heavenly,' she said, glancing at James. 'You're very fortunate to have Catherine to prepare all this for you.'

'She's been with us for years.' James helped himself to bread and added a generous helping of butter. 'She only comes in during the weekdays, because she has a family of her own to look after, but she always leaves food for us to tuck into over the weekend—home-made pies, casseroles, rice dishes and the like. Of course, my grandfather eats like a bird these days, so it's down to the rest of us to polish it off.'

He looked across the table at his grandfather and saw that he had finished with his food and was leaning back in his chair, dozing quietly. James's mouth made a faint curve. 'See what I mean? He must have had all of one chicken drumstick and a piece of bread, and that's it.'

'Is there no help to be had for his condition?' Louise was sad to see the old man looking so fragile.

James shook his head. 'I'm afraid not. The doctors have done everything they can for him with various medications, but his heart is worn out and the diuretics can only do so much to clear his lungs and lower his blood pressure. We just have to make sure that he isn't stressed in any way, and see to it that he takes things easy.'

'I'm sorry.'

He nodded. 'So am I. But I guess he's had a good life, and certainly he's seen to it that the estate is preserved in a way that honours tradition and keeps it within the bounds of what we can manage. He's never been one for bringing about change.'

He saw that she had laid down her fork. 'Have some fruit salad and cream,' he said. 'I think you'll find it's out of this world. We produce some of the fruit in our own greenhouses, and we have apples in season, and of course much of the food we eat is taken from our crops—peppers, cucumbers, and all the salad vegetables.'

'Do you have your own kitchen garden as well?'

'We do. We grow vegetables in one section, and then there's a herb garden. As soon as we've finished eating, I'll show you around.'

'Thanks, I'd like that.'

A short time later, when they were both replete, James got to his feet and held out a hand to bring her from her seat. 'Are you ready?' he asked.

'I am,' she said, hesitating momentarily. 'But what about your grandfather? Will he be all right left out here on his own?'

'I'll ask Catherine to keep an eye on him. She'll watch over him from the kitchen window, and come out to him from time to time.'

'All right.' She accepted the hand he offered, but as his palm closed firmly around hers she was startled by the sudden jolt of awareness that ran through her. It was as though the warmth of his grasp transmitted some elemental force that surged through her entire body, and when he followed that by placing a hand in the small of her back, she was done for.

She hadn't expected to feel the ripple of heat that raced through her bloodstream like wildfire, and it took a moment or two to recover her senses.

'Are you all right?'

'Yes, thank you.' She steadied herself, glad of his supporting arm just then, because her limbs were weak and there was a dizziness in her head that she couldn't account for. What on earth was wrong with her?

'Are you sure?' His expression was quizzical, but he wasn't letting go of her, and that in itself was adding to her problems.

'I'm sure,' she said, her voice husky. 'I think perhaps I must have stood up too quickly.'

'Hmm. Or maybe the sun is too strong at this time of day. Let's go inside and I'll show you around the place.'

Just in case, he put up a sun umbrella for Joseph before he stopped by the kitchen to ask Catherine to watch out for his grandfather, and then he set about showing her the rest of the Manor House. By now, Louise had recovered herself enough to absorb the beauty of her surroundings, and she was struck by the sumptuous quality of the décor and the stylish way in which the rooms had been laid out.

The emphasis throughout was on simplicity, but the furnishings were luxurious and every antique chair or table was carved with exquisite skill, adding to the atmosphere of age-old quality.

'I had no idea that you possessed such a heritage,' Louise murmured as they walked through each of the rooms and mounted the wide curving staircase. 'It's amazing to think that this has been home to your family for generation after generation. You must be so proud to belong here.'

'I suppose I am. Though I'm probably the first of my family to break away from tradition. I wanted to follow a career and practise medicine rather than become Lord of the Manor.'

She sent him a swift glance. 'Has that caused problems for you?'

They were standing in what must be the master bedroom, and she could see that this had been completely redesigned, with modern furnishings that blended perfectly with the period architecture. There was a four-poster bed, with silk curtains drawn back to form an attractive swirl of material.

'Not so much, up to now. My father wanted me to follow him in running the estate when my grandfather handed over the reins, but he didn't live to see me go against his wishes. My parents died almost fifteen years ago. They both succumbed to a nasty virus that they caught when they were travelling overseas.'

Her eyes clouded. 'I'm so sorry.'

He nodded acknowledgement of that, and showed her into another room. 'In a way, I think their loss helped me to make up my mind about becoming a doctor. It showed me how fragile the human body is and made me want to learn how to put things right.'

He waved a hand around the room. 'This is my grandfather's area in the centre of the house. My brother has his own suite of rooms in the west wing and I have the east side of the house, where we've just come from. Gemma prefers to live in the barn conversion with her family.'

He glanced at his watch. 'I'd show you the rest of the house, but we probably don't have time to do it all if we're to head back to the hospital in readiness for your shift.'

'That's okay.' So the room with the four-poster bed was his? Louise was still trying to take that in as they headed towards the stairs once more.

She wasn't at all sure how she felt about knowing where he slept. Just imagining him waking up in that huge bed was enough to send her hormones into a feverish frenzy. It wasn't like her at all to react in this way. It must be the house that was having this effect on her. Nothing else could account for it, surely?

She shook her head briefly in an attempt to clear it. 'How does your grandfather feel about you taking up medicine, instead of taking on the management of the estate?'

James shrugged. 'I think he was fairly philosophical about it, on the whole. He has always put his energy into doing what he felt was right, and medicine is one subject that he feels strongly about. That's why he funded the paediatric wing at the Royal Forest Hospital.'

Louise came to a sudden halt. 'He did?'

She reached for the balustrade and steadied herself. Then she stared up at him as the impact of what he had said began to dawn on her.

'His young nephew was treated there after he contracted meningitis. A paediatric specialist took care of the boy, and my grandfather was tremendously grateful to him for the way he looked after the child and for managing to save his life. After that, he wanted to make sure that the children in the surrounding area had a dedicated team to take care of them. Before his intervention, they were treated in the adult A&E department, but now they have the attention of doctors who specialise in paediatrics to care for them.'

Louise swallowed hard against the dryness of her throat. 'I can't believe that I didn't know any of this.' She closed her eyes briefly. 'No wonder you favour the Royal Forest Hospital in the new plans for the region. How am I supposed to fight this battle when everything is stacked up against me?'

His grey gaze travelled over her, capturing her troubled expression and moving to linger on the vulnerable curve of her mouth. 'Don't try to fight it,' he said softly. 'Accept that these things happen, and let me find you a place at the Royal Forest Hospital where you'll be appreciated.'

He reached out to her, winding a stray tendril of her silky hair around his fingers. She felt the brush of his hand against her cheek, soft as the touch of gossamer, beguiling her to give in and let him take over.

She pulled in a deep shaky breath. 'I can't do that,' she said in a ragged tone. 'My A&E unit means everything to me. I won't let it go.'

Even as she said it, her mind was in a whirl. Somehow, James had managed to work his way into her consciousness, making her aware of his every move, his closeness and gentle manner disrupting her cosy world and leading her to wonder whether somewhere she was missing out on something deep and meaningful.

Was she ready for a relationship? Why was it that work took over, leaving her no time to experience what everyone around her took for granted?

The trouble was, she was afraid to get close to him. She had dedicated the last few years to building up her children's unit, and he had the power to take it away from her.

CHAPTER SIX

'I WAS hoping to see how the little boy, Matthew, was doing, but it looks as though he's been moved from the intensive care unit.' Louise watched anxiously as the nurse at the central desk checked the computer screen. 'Does that mean his condition's improving?'

'I'm afraid not.' The nurse frowned as she read the case notes. 'He's the infant who swallowed antihistamine tablets, isn't he? He's still very poorly, but apparently they needed the bed for a more urgent case so he was taken to the side ward along the corridor.'

'I'll go and look in on him,' Louise murmured. 'Thanks.'

At least she was prepared for what she might find, and when she entered the ward she saw that the little boy was lying in the bed, unmoving, his eyes closed so that she could see the silk of his eyelashes against his cheeks. The strands of his hair lay in faintly damp swirls against his forehead. He was feverish, and the knowledge that he was still so desperately ill brought a lump to her throat.

She guessed that the staff were doing everything they could to alleviate the damage caused by the poison in his system, but the cardiac monitor showed that he was still struggling, and his temperature was raised, causing more problems.

'They say that he's having some trouble breathing,' his mother told her. 'They told me that the tablets he swallowed caused all sorts of things to go wrong. I feel so terrible. I put the tablets away in a cabinet, thinking that they would be safe in there, but he dragged a stool into the bathroom and climbed up to reach them.'

'I'm sorry. Children can be quite determined when they want to explore. All I can tell you is that everything possible is being done for him. Is your husband here to support you through all this?'

She nodded. 'He's gone to make a phone call. The grandparents are worried sick.'

'I can imagine they must be.'

Louise spoke to the mother for a while longer, but then she had to go back to A&E and prepare for the day ahead.

As soon as she walked into the unit, she knew that something was wrong. Nurses and doctors were gathered around the desk in the central area.

'Have you seen this?' Alice said, holding up the daily newspaper. 'There's a whole feature on the options put forward by the hospital Trust for the changes in the region's delivery of health care. Guess which option the Trust favours.'

'Let me see.'

Alice handed her the paper and Louise skimmed the article. 'I knew they would choose closure rather than anything else. There's a huge push to centralise everything. It makes me so cross.'

'Have you spoken to James about any of this since your meeting with the executives last week?' Alice asked.

'Only briefly.' Louise was still trying to take in the rest of the article.

'Spoken to me about what?' James enquired, coming out from the nearby waiting-room and walking over to them at the nurses' station.

Louise stiffened. 'You don't even get to have three guesses.' She waved the newspaper under his nose. 'They're quoting you in here, using phrases like "rational planning", "enhancing the quality of provision", and "inevitable change".'

She walked away from the desk, not wanting to involve the rest of the staff in this discussion, and James followed. Soon the group that was gathered around the central area broke up as people drifted back to their duties.

'I see nothing wrong with telling it how it is.' James didn't seem to be at all put out by her annoyance, and his calmness riled her all the more.

Louise pressed her lips together. 'What they should have said was that this reeks of cut-backs and downsizing and a reduction in the quality of care. But then, we weren't asked for our opinion, were we? This is all executive decision-making, followed by a concentrated public relations exercise, and yet the public have no idea what it's really all about, do they? They just swallow your medicine and believe you when you tell them you know best.'

'Nothing has been decided yet.' James raised a dark brow as though to imply she was blowing things out of all proportion. 'All the proposals have to be put out to public consultation.'

'And we all know which option you're promoting as the best one, don't we?' Louise glared at him. 'And we know why you've opted for that one too, yet there's no mention in the interview of the fact that your grandfather funded the wing at the Royal Forest Hospital, is there?'

'That would be because this reorganisation of the Trust's Health Services doesn't have anything to do with that. It's to do with putting the resources in the right place where they can benefit most people.'

'Is it? Is it really?' Her mouth made a grim line. 'We'll see about that, won't we? I think you'll find that when I've finished, the wider public will have a much better idea of what's actually going on.'

'That sounds as though you have something planned.' His gaze meshed with hers. 'What would that be, I wonder? A counter campaign?'

'Too right,' she bit out. 'You're not the only one who can speak to the press. "Hands off our hospital"—how's that for a headline? By the time I've finished, people will know exactly what closing down the paediatric A&E will mean to them and the wider community.'

James shrugged his shoulders, and she guessed that nothing of what she said disturbed him. Of course he wasn't concerned by what she had to say. He was wealthy and powerful, and he met with the chiefs of the Trust on a regular basis. She was just a feather blowing in the wind, and he could bat her away any time he felt like it.

Except that Louise was not about to give in so easily, and he would discover just how fierce an opponent she could be when she set her mind to it.

'I have to go to work,' she said in a tight voice, checking the board for her list of patients. 'We have a boy coming in—he had a fall from a bike and suffered possible internal injuries from landing on the handlebars.'

'That sounds nasty.' He studied her. 'Have you thought any more about the possibility of my joining you in the department on a temporary basis? I think it could be beneficial to both of us, and I could make a start right away. Or is that completely out of the question now?' His mouth made a wry twist.

Of course he was expecting her to shut him out. 'You think, because I'm a woman, that I'm bound to be prone to emotional highs and lows and I couldn't possibly be expected to make a decision based on simple logic, don't you?'

Her gaze narrowed on him and he made a vaguely non-committal gesture in return. 'I know how you feel about the situation,' he murmured. 'We're on opposite sides of the fence, and I suppose it's only natural that you would let your judgement be swayed by that.'

She glowered at him. 'I'm also in charge of the A&E unit and I'd be a fool to turn down any offer of qualified help, wouldn't I?' She sighed, making an effort to calm herself down. 'As a matter of fact, I had made up my mind to talk to you about that today. I checked you out, and you were right when you said that you might be overqualified. You specialised in both A&E and paediatrics, didn't you? Which makes it all the more surprising that you stepped down from practising full-time medicine to go into management. We need people with your expertise working with patients.'

'We also need people who can see the bigger picture and make changes that will improve the services we provide.'

Her mouth flattened. 'Perhaps it's best if we don't get into that argument again.' She waved a hand towards the board and its list of patients waiting to be seen. 'As soon as you've signed the relevant forms, the job's yours. Who knows, you might even begin to appreciate why we need this department to stay in its entirety.'

A flicker of amusement glimmered in his grey eyes. 'There is that,' he agreed, but she knew full well he was merely humouring her.

He might well be here to spy on her and gather fuel for his arguments, but it made no odds to her. She would fight him, and in the meantime she would reap the benefit of having one more skilled doctor on her team.

James went off to see the secretary in the human resources department, while Louise made her way to the ambulance bay to receive her patient.

Dean Wainwright, she discovered, was a gangling twelve-year-old boy who was doing his best to be brave. There were abrasions to his face and arms and, from the state of his trousers, she guessed that his knees were grazed too.

'The paramedic tells me that you came off your bike and fell on the handlebars,' Louise said as he was being wheeled to the treatment room. 'Is that right?'

He nodded. She could see that his face was tear streaked from the pain he was suffering, but he was doing his best to fight it. 'I was racing down the path on the common with my mates, and I hit a rock that was lying on the ground. It sort of tipped me sideways, and then Joey rammed into me, and I somersaulted onto the bike handle.'

Louise winced. 'And how did Joey come out of all this? Is he in the same state as you are?'

'Nah.' He pulled a face as his movements caused him pain. 'He's fine. He landed on the grass.'

'Well, Dean, I need to examine you, to see exactly what the damage is, and then I'll get a nurse to come and clean up some of these cuts for you. Can you show me where it hurts? I'll be as gentle as I possibly can.'

He pointed to his abdomen, and when she carefully checked him out she discovered that there was tenderness in the upper quadrant. 'Do you have pain anywhere else?' she asked.

'My left shoulder,' he said, 'but I didn't land on my shoulder. I don't remember doing anything to it.'

'It sometimes happens like that,' she told him. In

fact, she was pretty sure that he was feeling referred pain that was associated with blood in the abdomen irritating the diaphragm and the phrenic nerve.

'What we need to do now,' she said, 'is to have your cuts cleaned and then send you for a CT scan. That will give us an idea of what's going on inside. I'm going to give you an injection to take away the pain, and all you need to do is lie still and rest.'

She gave him the injection a moment later and then left him in Jenny's care while she drew the parents to one side in order to speak to them privately.

'How bad is it?' his father asked. 'He seems to be hurting quite badly.'

'He'll feel better in a moment or two when the injection begins to work,' she told him. 'It's possible that he has injured his spleen in the fall. I'm going to do a CT scan to find out what the damage is, and then we'll decide from there how to deal with it.'

For now, the parents were satisfied to sit back and wait for the results, but Louise was worried that the boy's injuries might be more severe than they had at first thought.

'You look concerned,' James said to her when he came back to A&E some time later.

She was looking at the pictures of Dean's injury, and now she pointed them out to James. 'It isn't looking too good, is it?' she said in a low tone.

'He might get away with a repair operation,' he remarked, studying the films. 'I suppose it all depends what the surgeon makes of it.'

Louise nodded. 'I'll call him, and in the meantime I'll go and have another word with the parents.' She sent him a quick glance. 'I take it you've signed everything that needs to be signed?'

'I have. The secretary is going to give you a ring to confirm that, any time now.'

'Good. Under normal circumstances you'd be treated to an induction day, but I dare say that would be irrelevant in your case.' Her mouth curved. 'It might be a good idea for you to pair up with Tim for the next couple of weeks and, if there's anything you want to know, I'm usually around.'

He returned her smile. 'I'll hunt you down if I need anything.'

Somehow, Louise had the feeling that was more of a threat than a promise. She told herself that she wasn't going to let him get to her, and went in search of the boy's parents once more.

Mr and Mrs Wainwright were visibly shaken when she told them that Dean needed surgery. 'I knew something was badly wrong,' the boy's mother said. 'He couldn't move for a while after he fell.' She looked anxiously at Louise. 'Is this the sort of operation that's done all the time?'

'The surgeon will have done lots of these operations,' Louise told her. 'Quite often, though, the spleen will heal itself without any intervention, provided that the patient rests completely for some time and then takes it easy over the following weeks. In Dean's case, I don't believe that will work. We really need to repair the tear.'

'He won't lose his spleen, will he?' Mr Wainwright asked. 'I've heard that it's bad if that happens.'

'The spleen helps us to fight infection,' Louise explained, 'and that's why doctors prefer not to remove it if it's at all possible. As I've said, in your son's case, it's not very likely that it will heal with rest alone, but the surgeon will look at the scans and decide what is best to be done. I think he'll most likely want to patch it up.'

Once she was sure that they understood the situation, Louise left them and went to attend to her other patients. There were a number of casualties brought in by ambulance, and it was almost lunch time before the hectic pace began to ease off a little.

She saw that James was in one of the treatment rooms administering nebulised medication to a little boy who was suffering from an asthma attack.

'I'm going to give him steroid therapy, along with intravenous antibiotics,' he was telling the mother, who was sitting by the bedside. 'He's feverish and we need to do tests to find out what type of infection it is that we're dealing with. The antibiotic that I'm giving him is a powerful one, but we may need to change that when we get the results. In the meantime, I think you'll find his breathing will improve in a little while.'

'Thank you, Doctor. He looks so much better already.'

James nodded, and Louise couldn't help but admire the gentle way in which he treated the little boy. He coaxed him into accepting the nebuliser mask, and his quiet, friendly manner seemed to help the child to relax. The boy seemed to be recovering, even as she watched.

Seeing James with the child made her heart fill with warmth and she stood for a moment, not saying anything, just drinking in the moment. What was it about this man that made her feel everything as though it was new and wonderful? Why was she always at loggerheads with him when he had such special qualities that took her breath away?

James left the treatment room a few minutes later, and Louise said quietly, 'I thought you were very good with that little boy. It's always very frightening when a child can't breathe properly, and it makes all the difference when you handle it in a calm manner.'

'I'm just thankful to see that his blood oxygen level is rising.'

'It looks as though he's going to be all right.' She smiled. 'I was thinking about the possibility of going to get something to eat while there's a lull. Perhaps you ought to do the same.'

Just then, Alice came over to them. 'James,' she said, 'someone's here to see you. He's waiting by the main doors.'

James looked where she indicated, and excused himself.

'They look so much alike, don't they?' Alice murmured, glancing over to where James stood with the visitor, and Louise had to agree. The men were both tall and lean, with black hair cut in a short neat style.

'Dishy's not the word, is it?' Alice murmured. 'It

doesn't do either of them justice, does it? See, I've come over all hot and bothered now.' She pretended to fan her cheeks and Louise laughed.

'Perhaps you'd better go and splash your face with cold water,' she said.

'Yeah, right.' Alice went back to work, leaving Louise to wonder if this was James's brother who had come to talk to him.

Perhaps he had noticed her glance, because James turned to her and beckoned her over to him. 'Do you have a minute to come and say hello to my brother, Robert?'

She went over to them and held out her hand to the man. 'I thought I could see a resemblance.' He looked as though he was younger than James, and that prompted her to say, 'I hadn't expected there to be much age difference between you since you're managing the estate, but I gather you must be the younger brother?'

Robert nodded. 'There are around five years between us. Gemma is the middle one. I guess that makes me the baby.' He grinned, and Louise smiled in return.

'Robert has just dropped by to give me news of my grandfather. I was just about to take him over to the doctors' lounge so that we could talk for a while.'

'Yes, of course. That's a good idea.' She sent Robert a quick look. 'How is your grandfather?'

His expression sobered. 'Not good, I'm afraid. Gemma's staying with him at the moment so that I could come into town and order some supplies. It's all been a bit of a rush, really, sorting things out. I had to call the doctor in earlier today, and he was talking about admitting him to hospital. Of course, Grandad won't hear of it.'

'That must be difficult for you.'

'It is, though I understand why he digs his heels in. I think I would probably do the same, if I were his age.'

She nodded. 'I suppose we all prefer the comfort of home and family when we're ill.' Stepping back a little, she said, 'I'll leave you two to talk, then.'

To James, she added, 'You should offer your brother some food from the trolley.' And then, glancing at Robert, she murmured, 'I don't suppose you've had time to eat if you've been rushing about, have you?'

'That's true,' he agreed. 'Lately, meals seem to get slotted in wherever I get the chance.'

James chuckled. 'Louise has this wonderful trolley full of goodies, so that the staff can help themselves to food whenever they feel hungry. She maintains that people can't work properly when their blood sugar is low, and so they can snack whenever they like.'

'Whenever they can grab a free moment, more like. We're run off our feet here sometimes, and taking time out to eat a sandwich or a doughnut can make all the difference to your energy levels and how you feel about the job.'

James sent her an assessing look. 'And, for all that, she never puts an ounce on that gorgeous figure.'

Louise felt the colour rise in her cheeks. He had

noticed her figure? Did he really think she looked good? Why was it that he had the power to throw her off balance this way?

Robert smiled, and James tacked on, 'Why don't you come and join us for a while? You were talking about taking a break, weren't you, and as far as I know you haven't stopped yet today.'

Louise blinked and recovered from her reverie. Had he been taking note? Perhaps her thoughts about a spy in the camp weren't too far off base after all.

Even so, the idea of a short break from the rush of A&E was welcoming just then. 'Perhaps I will,' she murmured. 'I just need to make sure that the surgeon has been to look in on my patient, and then I'll come and find you.'

A few minutes later, she went to join them in the doctors' lounge. Perhaps her instincts were off base, but she thought she detected sparks in the atmosphere. Had the brothers been arguing? Helping herself to coffee from the filter jug, she studied the array of food on the trolley and picked out a sandwich.

Robert was telling James about his problems running the farm, and she gathered that he wasn't happy about the income that they were deriving from the estate.

'You have no idea what I'm up against,' he was saying. 'Or, if you do, you're closing your eyes to it.' He lowered his voice when he saw that Louise had entered the room, but her hearing was acute and she heard everything that was said.

'We could do so much better if Grandad would let

us open the house up to visitors,' Robert went on. 'As it is, the income we're getting from the farms is adequate, but not brilliant, when you consider all the ongoing repairs that have to be made. There is so much more that we could be doing.'

'Grandad has always been a traditionalist. You know that,' James murmured. He seemed unperturbed by his brother's dilemma. 'In a way, I can see his point. It's our home, and he doesn't want it invaded by the general public.'

'He's behind the times.'

'Maybe.'

They both fell silent as Louise came to sit with them at the table. 'James told me that one of the animals was sick,' she remarked, glancing towards Robert and feeling a little worried in case she was intruding. 'He said you had called in the vet. Is everything all right now?'

Robert nodded. 'One of the mares was in foal, and she was having some difficulty. The vet sorted things out, though, and now she has a healthy male offspring.'

'That's delightful.' She sent him a sparkling glance. 'You must be so pleased. Do you have many horses— I thought the stable block had been converted into houses? Perhaps I had that wrong.'

'No, it's true that most of these stables have been converted, but there was another smaller block that we kept for its original purpose. We have a couple of mares and a stallion. Nothing like in the old days, but then we don't use horses for farm work these days. Gemma likes to go out riding, and of course the children love the new foal.'

'I'm sure they do.' She took a bite out of her sandwich and then after a while she said, 'I expect that you're very busy, managing such a large estate. It can't be easy to do that.'

'Well, it would be difficult at the best of times, but I have to abide by my grandfather's wishes, and he has his own way of doing things. It isn't always the best way, in my opinion.'

'Wouldn't it make a difference if you and James put up a united front?'

Robert made a brief, cool smile. 'We have tried, but to no avail. Anyway, I think James secretly agrees with Grandad, so he doesn't try too hard to sway him.'

He swallowed the last of his coffee and put down his cup. 'Still, one day it will be James's problem. He's next in line to inherit the title and, being head of the family, he'll be the one who has to work out the best way of doing things.' He glanced at his brother. 'I'm not sure how that will go down, when his main interest is medicine.'

James grimaced, and Louise said cautiously, 'Do I detect some friction here?'

'I don't think so,' James answered. 'Robert and I rub along well enough.'

Robert's mouth made a rueful shape. 'That may be true, but you're burying your head in the sand, just the same as Grandad. I'm warning you, brother—one of these days you're going to have to take it on board.'

Robert stood up. 'I have to get back. I've ordered the new fencing and loaded up the car with equipment, and now I need to go and see how Gemma's doing. She told me she was hoping to get back to the gallery for a couple of hours.' He held out a hand to Louise. 'It's been good meeting you,' he said.

James went with him, seeing him out, and Louise lingered over her coffee for a while, wondering just how deep the problems went within the family. Was there some resentment on Robert's part because he was left to deal with the estate?

A few minutes later, she went to the central desk to look over her patients' charts, and James came to join her.

'He was anxious to get back to the Manor and check on Grandad,' he said.

'I hope he'll find that he's not doing too badly.' She sent him a fleeting look. 'Do you think you'll be able to smooth things over with your brother?'

'Why should I need to do that?'

Louise gave a diffident shrug. 'I thought I sensed a problem between you two.' She studied him, a frown knotting her brow. 'Perhaps I was wrong. After all, what would I know of sibling rivalry?'

'Do you think that's the case with me and Robert?'

'I didn't mean to intrude on you, but you invited me to join you and I couldn't help noticing that there was some slight tension in the air. It seemed to stem from the problem of who does what and who has overall control.'

'Robert is entitled to say what he thinks. He's right, in a way. It's a heritage I'm not ready for, and he knows it.'

'Is that why you went overseas—to escape?'

'I didn't see it that way, at the time.' He looked at her directly. 'I can see that my brother needs help, but I'm not sure that I'm the one to give it. My calling is medicine. It has been that way for a long time, and I suppose I'm torn between that and my heritage.'

'So now you're not doing either to any great extent.' She studied his proud features, taking note of his strong jaw line, the well-defined arch of his cheekbones. 'I can understand how Robert must feel. You've always had it easy, haven't you? Your brother has put in all this hard work to keep the estate running smoothly, just the same as I've put in all this effort to build up my unit, and it looks as though we're both at the mercy of the people who have the power to interfere. You tried to turn your back on your heritage, but you should be glad of those family ties.'

She frowned. 'I don't have any, and it makes me sad to see you throwing yours away with scarcely a thought for the consequences.'

'You don't know anything about my family or the way we operate.' His gaze pierced her, laser-sharp, his eyes darkening to a flinty grey. 'We've always dealt perfectly well with whatever came our way and I see no reason why that should change. My brother's happy enough with his role. A few negative comments don't signify anything.'

'Maybe not,' she said. He was angry with her, and she could see that she had touched on a chord that jangled his nerves. If everything was going so smoothly, why was he so riled? 'I'm just saying that I think you should be prepared for problems ahead.'

His mouth tightened. Then he drew out a file from the tray and walked away from her without uttering another word.

Louise watched him go. Had she gone too far? It had always been in her nature to speak her mind, but where should she draw the line? Somehow, over the past week, she had come to care deeply about James and his family. It mattered to her that things should go smoothly for them, and yet, if anyone had asked her why that was, she would have been at a loss to explain.

Had James managed to work his way into her heart? A sea change was happening, and only now was she starting to question how her life had been taken over by work. Up till now, she had been content, happy just to be with the children who came into her care, but suddenly her world was shifting, and all at once she was beginning to feel that some vital part was missing from her life.

CHAPTER SEVEN

'SAVE our A&E.' The protestors, an assorted bunch of people from all walks of life—men, women, young and old—held their placards high and milled about in front of the hospital.

'Don't let them close us down.' The doctors and nurses were out in force to add their points of view.

'Do you want to travel thirty or forty miles to the nearest hospital when your child has been injured in a traffic accident?' someone shouted.

A woman took up the call. 'What will happen to your child if he's having an asthma attack and there's no paediatric A&E locally?'

Press photographers were taking snapshots of the scene, and Louise noticed that a TV cameraman was moving in to get a close-up of the crowd.

Then James appeared, and a young woman came and held a microphone up to him, saying, 'This is prime time regional news. James Ashleigh—you've put your name to this call for closure. What do you say to these people who are frightened for the lives of their children?'

He looked into her eyes, and Louise knew a wave of irritation as the young woman's cool veneer melted under the warmth of his smile just as though the sun had come out in all its glory.

'I want you to know that I do understand everyone's concern,' he said, his voice lilting, melodic in its gentle tone. 'Our aim as doctors is, and always has been, to save lives. But the fact is, local is not always best. We are trying to create regional hospitals that will provide the very best in care—expert care. Some treatments are by their nature more complex than others, and these will be provided in the new refurbished wing at the Royal Forest Hospital.'

'But what will happen to those youngsters who are injured and need treatment right away?' To give her credit, the girl stayed on target, and Louise cautiously revised her opinion of her.

'There will be local casualty units available,' he said. 'You already have the walk-in centre just four miles from here, but under the plans we're putting forward there will be another small unit created at the hospital.'

The protesters, quiet until now, suddenly erupted. 'He's talking about minor injuries,' a man shouted. 'Who's going to take proper care of our kids? Answer me that.'

James was speaking once more, in that measured, amicable tone that he had used before, and in spite of herself Louise couldn't help but admire him for his calm way of dealing with these people. He couldn't have known that they would be lying in wait outside the hospital, but he'd handled the situation with his usual assured style. She decided that she had seen enough.

'Thank you for helping me to organise this,' she said, going over to one of the campaign leaders. 'I have to go and get back to work, but I wanted to tell you that you've done really well, arranging such a massive turnout.'

He nodded. 'This is just the beginning. We have all sorts of actions up our sleeves. I just hope that they show your interview in full on TV,' he said. 'You were brilliant. You put in a strong case for keeping the unit.'

'Thanks for that. I hope it's done some good.'

But now she had to get back to work. First on her list of things to do was the daily meeting with staff to check on patients they had seen the day before. They would organise follow-up measures to be taken, and make sure that letters had been sent to GPs.

'How is Dean Wainwright doing?' she asked, and Alice flicked through the notes.

'He had a successful repair operation. He's been admitted to the surgical ward for rest and observation. He seems to be doing fine.'

'That's great. Is there any news of young Matthew, the child who swallowed the antihistamine tablets?'

Alice shook her head. 'Nothing encouraging, really. He's still in a worrying condition.'

The news was upsetting. Louise braced herself to go on with her work and a few minutes later she wound up the meeting. Then she went in search of her next patient.

Unexpectedly, she came face to face with James as she walked towards the treatment room.

'Was that meant to be a baptism of fire?' he asked. His jaw was set at a hard angle and she guessed he wasn't best pleased by his reception. She suffered a small qualm when she remembered how they had parted in discord the previous day, but she couldn't afford to let her emotions get in the way.

'So you survived the onslaught, did you? I'm so glad.' She gave him a quick smile. 'Sorry about that, but someone has to put forward the opposite point of view. We can't have you having everything your own way, can we?'

'Heaven forbid,' James said in a laconic tone. 'That would make life just too easy, wouldn't it? Still, I expect you know how much I relish a challenge, so it was thoughtful of you to set that up for me.' His grey eyes glittered, homing in on her, and Louise felt a frisson of awareness run along her spine.

'Anything to oblige,' she murmured. 'But now I have to get on with my work.' She scanned her patient's case notes and then frowned. 'Poor mite. I'd better go and see what I can do for this six-year-old. I have her on oxygen, but she's very tired and weak. I'm thinking she'll need steroid therapy to support her immune system. She's coughing up blood and passing it in her urine too, from the looks of these lab results.'

James quickly lost any hint of antagonism and became immediately on the alert. 'Then I guess she must be anaemic, too. Are you checking for Goodpasture's syndrome?'

Louise nodded. 'The findings are all pointing that

way, so we need to act quickly if she's not to progress to renal failure. I've cross-matched her blood and I think she'll need a transfusion of red blood cells. I'm going to admit her and call for a specialist consultation.'

No sooner had she done that, and arranged for the child to be transferred to a ward, than the department was thrown into a feverish bout of activity.

'We've patients coming in from a traffic accident,' Alice told her. 'A lorry swerved across the dual carriageway and three cars were caught up in the smash. There are several casualties, including six children. A five-year-old with chest trauma is the most badly injured. He'll be here any moment now. It's looking pretty bad.'

'Okay. Call the trauma team and include James in that. Find Ryan, and ask him to do triage. Alice, I want you and Jenny to sort out treatment rooms and prepare everything we need. I'll gather up Tim and any of the Senior House Officers that we can spare and allocate patients to them.'

She was already on the move and, when her small patient was rapidly wheeled in a few minutes later, she directed Andy, the paramedic, to take him to the nearest resuscitation room.

The boy was in a shocking state, with a barely palpable pulse and open wounds to his chest. There were signs of contusions to the lungs as well as bleeding within the chest cavity. An overwhelming feeling of dread washed over her. Then her professional instinct kicked in, and she blocked everything out except the need to keep him alive.

She worked quickly to secure his airway with an endotracheal tube, afterwards stepping to one side so that Jenny could take over with the oxygen.

'His blood pressure is falling fast, and I'm hearing muffled heart tones. The neck veins are distended.' Louise continued with her examination, and each finding made her all the more anxious for this little boy's safety.

'He's going into shock. We need to get some lines in and start volume replacement right away.' Almost before she had finished speaking, James was working to set that up.

A short time later he said, 'I've given him two fluid boluses of lactated Ringer's solution, but he's still not responding. He must still be losing blood from somewhere, and it can't simply be from the lung.'

'We'll have to transfuse him.'

'I'm on it.' Jenny was preparing the packs of blood for transfusion.

Louise glanced at James and said on an urgent note, 'I'm going to try to get to the source of the bleeding. The scans are showing blood pooling around the heart, so I need to get to it fast, but I'm worried about his lung injury. Will you put in a tube to the lung and drain the haematoma? That should bring his oxygen level up.'

'I'm already there.' He was readying the equipment as she spoke, and Louise was relieved to see that the team around her was working well. Now her main concern was to find the source of the bleeding and put a stop to it.

Just a few moments later, she discovered a small puncture wound in the child's heart, along with damage to the blood vessels. 'Alice,' she said urgently, 'put your finger here and keep pressure on the hole until I can put a catheter in place.'

The catheter would help to control the bleeding and, as soon as that was in position, she set about clamping the damaged blood vessels around the heart.

'You'll want to suture the lacerations?' Alice was readying herself to hand over the necessary equipment.

'Yes, I'll use polypropylene sutures for the heart itself.' She briefly checked the monitors, desperately worried that they were running out of time. How long could this child survive if his heart was so badly injured?

'Shall I start on the blood vessel sutures?' James asked. 'I'll do horizontal mattress sutures reinforced with pledgets.'

'Thanks.' She sent a quick glance to the young Senior House Officer who was assisting. 'Work with James,' she said quietly, 'and you'll be able to see how it's done.'

They worked together, relying on the support of the rest of their colleagues to keep a check on the child's status and make sure that he was adequately anaesthetised.

Louise had finished putting in the sutures and was assessing the child's circulation when a nurse from a neighbouring treatment room rushed in. 'Ryan needs you next door,' she said in a breathless voice.

'His patient's collapsing and he's having trouble stabilising her.'

Louise glanced at James. 'Would you be able to take over here?'

He nodded. 'I'm doing the last of the sutures now. You go ahead.'

She hurried out of the room and went to see what was happening with the child in Ryan's care.

'I've been treating her for a fractured arm, but suddenly her condition has deteriorated. The CT scans haven't shown anything amiss, and I can't account for why this is happening.'

'Have you done an abdominal examination?'

'Yes, I did all the usual checks.'

'Something might have developed since then. I'll do another, just to be sure.' Louise examined the little girl and said cautiously, 'There seems to be some distension in the abdomen now. We'll do a peritoneal lavage to see if there's any bleeding.'

A short time later, she had isolated a source of bleeding and the child was referred for immediate surgery. Louise went back to the main thoroughfare and checked to see how her colleagues were coping.

'I think we have it all under control now,' Tim, the Specialist Registrar, told her. 'All our patients have come through the initial stages okay.' He looked around at the assembled staff, a brow raised in query, and there was a general nod of agreement.

'That's brilliant work. Well done, everyone.' Louise smiled, and checked her watch. 'I'm going to freshen up, and then I'll look in on the overdose patient upstairs while we have a lull. You'd better all take turns in going for a break while you have the chance.'

She caught sight of James, as he removed his waterproof coverall and tossed it into a bin. A fleeting smile touched his mouth as he returned her gaze. She had to acknowledge that he had been a tremendous asset to her in their attempts to keep the five-year-old boy alive. Would the outcome have been the same if he hadn't been there to help?

A wave of weariness washed over her, and for a moment or two she couldn't fathom why she was feeling this way. The concentrated efforts of the last few hours seemed to have taken more out of her than she had expected.

Perhaps it was the knowledge that these children in her care might not have survived if they had been taken on the longer journey to the Royal Forest Hospital that was troubling her more than anything. In cases like these, time was of the essence, and small patients with injuries such as these needed expert attention within the hour if they were to have any chance of living through the trauma. Would new patients get that in the months to come if the hospital's Trust board had its way?

Needing to get away for a minute, she took the lift up to the medical ward. All was quiet and nurses moved around the area, adjusting drips here and there or administering medication as necessary. The children here were very sick, having been transferred from the intensive care unit, and Louise was careful not to disturb them.

Three-year-old Matthew was lying on his side, but his eyes were open and he was staring straight ahead at the pictures on a video screen that a nurse had provided for him. Monitors nearby recorded his vital signs, and Louise could see that he was still very poorly. His heart rate was fast, and his oxygen level was low, so that every now and again the equipment would bleep a warning and a nurse would come and check his condition.

He looked as though he was too weak to move. Even so, she was moved to smile as she watched him. The infant was holding onto a packet of crisps that lay on the bed in front of him and, as she looked on, he dipped one finger into the bag, pulling out a crisp. It was such a tiny, insignificant movement, but it showed so much, and it brought a lump to her throat. The boy was awake and ready to eat, even if it was only a crisp and he didn't have the energy to sit up.

There was a movement beside her and Louise glanced around, startled to see that James had come to join her. Maybe he, too, needed to reassure himself that the child was still holding onto life.

'He doesn't have the energy to move, does he?' she said softly. 'He looks exhausted.'

'That's true…' James murmured, 'but he's been through a tremendous battle, and I'd say he was on the mend at last, wouldn't you?'

Her smile widened. 'Oh, yes, I'd say so, definitely.'

James's arm went around her waist, a light, gentle touch that drew her close and showed they were in tune with one another, united in their joy that this tiny infant had conquered his illness against all the odds. The knowledge that he was on the road to recovery made her spirits soar…or it might have been that James's embrace was paramount in promoting her newfound happiness. He had an overwhelming power to revive her flagging morale.

It was such a companionable, casual, yet intimate caress and, for a while, neither of them moved. They had been through so much in these last few hours, had together faced one of the greatest tests they could ever know, and right now she was more than content to have him hold her this way.

Of course, she knew why he was keeping her close. It wasn't meant to be personal, was it? It was just that this was a special time, a moment to share.

Eventually, though, she knew that she had to come back down to the reality of everyday life. 'I suppose I should go back to A&E,' she said, a little sigh escaping her.

He nodded, letting his arm fall away from her, and she felt the loss of his touch as though a cool breeze had drifted over her skin.

'I was glad of your help this morning,' she told him as they left the ward. 'You were so competent in everything you did that it helped take some of the pressure from me, knowing that I could rely on you.'

'I would say that you were pretty spectacular yourself,' he said with a smile. 'I've never seen anyone so concentrated, so decisive about what needed to be done. If anyone pulled that child through, it was you.'

'It was a team effort,' she said. 'That's always the way things work best, when we all know our roles and can depend on one another.'

'Maybe, but you even found it in you to realise that there was a teaching situation in there. That young SHO was anxious about what was going on, but it helped for her to be able to take part and learn from what we were doing.'

He pushed open the exit door, one hand resting on the small of her back as he ushered her through to the corridor. Did he know the effect his touch had on her? Or was it simply a negligent gesture, a courtesy born of generations of aristocratic background and essential good manners?

She tried to shake off the cloud of sensation that fogged her brain. Getting to know him and respect him was playing havoc with her nervous system. How could she allow herself to grow fond of the man who might eventually destroy her career?

'How does it feel to be working in A&E?' she asked him. 'I expect it must feel strange to you after you've been spending so much time dealing with management issues. Is it likely to cut in on your role as an executive?'

He gave it some thought. 'It's more a question of having to rearrange my schedule,' he said after a moment or two. 'I don't mind doing that. I like to be busy, and it's good to be back in the fast-moving area of emergency medicine. The work that I've been used to in the renal unit is much less frantic, so I suppose I have to adjust more to the pace. I can always miss out on one or two management meetings as long as they are ones where I don't need to put in a vote. I have the minutes of the meetings to outline the gist of the discussions.'

'Do you ever have to make decisions about the management of the Ashleigh estate?' She hesitated, remembering how annoyed he had been by her comments the day before. But she had never been one to let troubles fester, and it seemed to her that he was heading for trouble if he ignored his brother's comments. 'It seemed to me that your brother would have liked a little more support.'

He sent her an oblique glance as he pressed the button for the lift, but he appeared to have put his anger behind him. 'I keep an overall view of the situation. Robert chose to take on the management role. He's always been interested in the land and different ways of farming. He might complain from time to time, but he's well suited to the job and up to now he's always been able to keep things running smoothly.'

'But the upkeep of the Manor can be daunting, can't it? He seemed to have some worries about whether you were getting the best out of the estate. It must be galling for him to have lots of ideas about changes that can be made, but to be vetoed at every turn.'

'We've never had to worry about that before. I doubt my grandfather would have funded the paediatric wing if it was a problem for him.' The lift doors swished open and they stepped inside, waiting until they were closed and the lift began to descend. 'I think Robert's trouble stems from the fact that he's looking to the future when he might want to settle down and have a family of his own. Perhaps he's trying to impress his fiancée.'

'Or perhaps he resents the fact that he's left to do it all on his own. It can be difficult putting everything into your career, only to find that it's in jeopardy.'

He shot her a penetrating stare. 'It seems to me that you're the one who has a problem with that. It isn't just the threat of closure that bothers you, is it? Is it that you're understaffed? Are you afraid that I'll leave you in the lurch and abandon my work here at the hospital? You seemed to be concerned that I might have overextended myself in some way.'

'No. That didn't enter my head. After all, you signed a contract, albeit a temporary one.' She frowned. 'I suppose I'm bewildered by the way you keep a foot in both camps. You have all the trappings of wealth and privilege, and yet you appear to have turned your back on the very thing that gave you all that. And you wanted to practise medicine, but discovered a higher cause in management and stepped away from what you thought had been your chosen career. None of it makes sense to me.'

She gave him a long, assessing look. 'If the truth were known, I think you're confused about what it is that you really want. You're in denial and that's why there's friction between you and your brother, and why you can't see how much harm you're doing in supporting the option for closure in favour of the Royal Forest

Hospital. You've lost sight of what makes people tick and how they need their smaller goals to be valued.'

The doors of the lift started to open and he pressed the button to close them again, shutting them away from prying eyes.

'Maybe you're the one who's lost sight of what it is to be flexible. You're only thinking about the way your unit will be affected because it means everything to you. You've put your life and soul into developing it, instead of looking to the outside world for fulfilment. How else do you account for the fact that it's like your second home?'

His grey gaze pierced her, becoming smoky in its intensity. 'Why aren't you married and looking after a family of your own? You'd be far less likely to be concerned about what happens here if you had your own children to look after.'

'How patronising is that? Where are your wife and family?'

He smiled as he conceded the hit. He stared down at her, moving in on her, so that there was scarcely any distance between them and she could feel the warmth emanating from his long body. Then he reached out to her, his hand making a slow sweep of her body from her ribcage to the soft swell of her hip and lingering there, so that a rush of heat filled her veins and raced around her body in a torrent of guilt-ridden desire.

'I'm not the one who has a problem,' he murmured.

'You're wrong,' she said, her voice ragged as she pulled in a shaky breath. 'You're a man, and because of that you're reducing everything to the lowest common denominator, confusing sex with a desire for job satisfaction and the reward of knowing that lives are being saved.' Her green eyes sparked. 'I might have known I couldn't reason with you. You don't know the meaning of the word.'

'Really? Are you sure about that?' His hand lifted, coming to rest momentarily on the curve of her cheek before trailing slowly along the line of her jaw. A glimmer started in the depths of his eyes and she held her breath, her body warring with her mind in the struggle to absorb the sensations he was invoking in her.

'I'm very sure,' she said, but her voice was husky and there was a betraying flicker in her throat as the pulse there began to beat to a hot, heavy rhythm.

He laughed softly, releasing her as suddenly as he had swooped, and she watched him, her eyes wide, her mind whirling as though she had stepped onto a spinning dais.

The lift doors opened and he walked out, stepping into the main thoroughfare without a backward glance, humming a tune to himself as though he didn't have a care in the world.

Louise stayed where she was, staring after him until her heartbeat settled down to something resembling normality once more.

He was the devil in a smart grey suit and just then she resented him with all her might. How could he do that to her? How could he make her blood tingle and her skin prickle and every nerve ending in her body burn with sheer unadulterated excitement and then simply walk away as though nothing had happened? He was a fiend.

CHAPTER EIGHT

'THERE'S a little girl sitting in the waiting-room with her mother,' Alice said, handing Louise a chart. 'Her name's Nicola Soulsby. She's five years old and I'm pretty sure she must be James's niece, but he isn't around just now. Do you want to take a look at her?'

Louise sent her a startled look. 'They're here? What's wrong with her? Has she had an accident?'

'A fall, from the sound of things, on to her arm. She's quite tearful so I guess it must be hurting her quite a bit, and of course her mother's worried. She didn't mention that she's James's sister, but I recognised her from the odd time she's dropped by to see James.'

'I'll take them through to the treatment room. Do we know where James is right now?'

'He's at a management meeting at the Royal Forest, as far as I know.' Alice made a face. 'They're talking through proposals to make the Royal Forest Hospital a "centre of excellence" from what I gather.' On a mischievous note, she tacked on, 'Shall I give him a ring and disturb him?'

Louise smiled ruefully. 'I think we'd better let him know that Nicola has hurt herself. He'd want to be told if his family is here.'

She was actually relieved that James was not around today. After the close encounter with him that day in the lift it had taken some time for her nerves to settle down. Every time he was anywhere near her, her senses went into overdrive and she was finding that working with him was far more difficult than she might have imagined. He was charming, easygoing and extremely good at his job, but having him nearby day after day was altogether too disconcerting for comfort.

She glanced at the chart and then went out to the waiting-room to greet Gemma and her daughter. 'I'm so sorry that you've had to come here, but I must say it's lovely to see you again.'

'And it's good to see you.' Gemma greeted her with a quick smile, but her expression was strained. 'I wish it wasn't under these circumstances. I'm afraid Nicola has hurt herself—there's some swelling around her elbow, so I thought we should come here and have it checked out. She was at a friend's party—they were holding the event at a roller skating rink and she fell awkwardly.'

Louise looked at the child. 'Well, I'm sorry that your party was cut short, Nicola. What a shame you had to come away.'

Nicola made a pout. 'Anne-Marie's still there.'

'Is she? Perhaps she'll bring you a goodie bag when she comes away.'

Nicola brightened a fraction at the thought.

'We'd better go through to the treatment room,' Louise suggested, 'so that I can take a look at your arm.' She led the way, adding, 'I think you'll like it in this room. I've put up the picture of the little puppy peeping out from the shrubs. Do you remember the picture from your mother's art gallery?'

Nicola nodded, and Louise said, 'He looks right at home in there with all the walls painted to look like a garden. Perhaps you'd like to look around and see if you can find all the animals that are hiding behind the trees and flowers.'

Nicola's eyes widened as they entered the room, and her tears seemed to have dried up for now. She gazed about her. 'There's a rabbit,' she said, pointing with her uninjured arm to where a fluffy creature was hidden behind tufts of meadow grass, looking longingly at a mouth-watering bed of carrots.

'So there is.' Louise smiled. 'Do you think you could climb up onto the bed here for me, poppet? Use these steps.'

Gemma helped her daughter to climb up, and Nicola continued to look around. She giggled. 'I can see a kitten over there. She's hiding in a plant pot.'

'She is.' Louise had already made a visual check of the child's arm, and now she said softly, 'I just need to see if you can wiggle your fingers and bend your arm for me.'

This was obviously uncomfortable for the child, and Louise said, 'All right, Nicola, you can rest now. What we need to do is to get some pictures of the bones inside your arm—it won't hurt at all to do that, but it will help us because we'll be able to see if everything is as it should be. Is that all right with you?'

Nicola nodded, and Louise turned her attention to Gemma. 'I don't think there's a fracture, but to make sure we'll take some X-ray pictures of the area around the elbow. It might be that there's a slight displacement of the joint, but that won't necessarily show up on the X-ray films. To be safe, we'll probably do an ultrasound scan afterwards, and that should tell us what we need to know.'

'Thanks,' Gemma said. 'Shall we go and get those done now?'

'Yes, I'll write out the forms for you to hand to the radiologist. Come back here when you've had them done, and I'll talk to you again.'

Mother and daughter went off together, and Louise went in search of her next patient.

Gemma was still in the radiology department when James arrived at the hospital a short time later.

'How's Nicola?' he asked, catching up with Louise in the central area as she arranged for another small patient to be taken over to the observation ward. 'Is she still here?'

'She's still with radiology. She's okay. I gave her a painkiller.'

He relaxed a fraction. 'That's good. I wasn't sure what to expect. Is Gemma bearing up okay?'

'She's fine. Your sister seems to be a very level-headed young woman.'

'Yes, she always has been.' He followed her over to

the desk. 'I see the protest marchers are out in force again at the front of the hospital. I'm beginning to think you arrange for them to be here specifically for when I'm coming into the department.'

'Of course I do,' she agreed, treating the comment with the sarcasm it deserved. She finished writing up her notes and dropped the patient's chart back into the tray. 'I made sure that they had a complete rundown of your timetable, along with that of the chief executive. How else am I to have any fun around here? We both know I don't have any family commitments to take up my time, don't we?'

'Yeah, right.' A hint of amusement played over his mouth. 'Not only are you keeping up the pressure, but you've brought the local Member of Parliament on board, haven't you? He was outside, talking to the press. I can't help wondering how exactly you managed to do that.'

'He's always been very sympathetic to our cause.'

'Oh, yes? Is there any particular reason for that?'

Her shoulders lifted. 'It might be something to do with the fact that we treated his daughter here, after she had an accident. He was very impressed with us, apparently.'

His mouth made a wry shape. 'I can imagine.' He studied her briefly, his glance moving over the gentle curves of her figure, outlined by the smoothly fitting skirt and stretch cotton top that she was wearing beneath her cream-coloured jacket. 'I'm also impressed by you for a number of reasons—for your dedication, and for the calm way you handle everything around here. Not to mention the fact that you brighten the place up.'

She sent him a vaguely dismissive stare. 'Were you born a flirt or did you just turn out that way?'

He laughed. 'I guess it comes naturally.' Glancing around the department, he sobered quickly enough. 'So Nicola's down in radiology—do you know what the damage is?'

'It wasn't clear from the X-ray films. I put a call through to the department, to find out, and they tell me her arm isn't fractured. They're doing an ultrasound scan for me, though, because I suspect the medial epicondyle is displaced.'

'Poor little scrap. Is she bearing up okay?'

'I think so. I put her arm in a temporary sling, but as soon as she comes back here I'll see to it that we help her to feel better.'

'Thanks, Louise. I'm glad you were able to look after her. Grandad will be pleased, too. He rang me to say that Gemma had to dash off to the skating rink to collect Nicola, and he wanted to know what was happening. As soon as I told him that you were taking care of her, he began to relax.'

'That's good to know. How is he?'

James's mouth made a downward curve. 'Not good, I'm afraid, but at least he still has all his mental faculties, even though his body is letting him down. He asked me to invite you to tea at the weekend. I think it's his way of thanking you for being there for the girls.'

'I'm just doing my job.'

'Yes, but it's the way you do it that pleases Grandad. Will you come to tea? We'd all like to see you there.'

She wondered if he truly meant that. Wasn't she a thorn in his side, causing him to explain his policies at every turn? And did she really fit in amongst his power-ful titled family, when their priorities were totally opposite to hers?

Still, although she had only known him for a short time, she did have a great fondness for his grandfather, and if he was the one issuing the invitation it would be churlish of her to refuse, wouldn't it?

'I'd like that, thank you.'

'That's great.' He leaned negligently against the desk, his long legs thrust out, one foot casually crossed over the other.

She looked away. He looked heart-meltingly good and she wished that her treacherous hormones would stop recognising that fact.

He said softly, 'After seeing the way you work here, I think it will do you a world of good to get away and relax for a while.'

She decided to cut him off at the pass. 'If you think it might make me more amenable to your plans, then I'm afraid you're setting yourself up for disappoint-ment.'

'Oh, I don't know about that.' His gaze narrowed on her, so that he was watching her through dark, secre-tive eyes that smouldered with promise. 'At least it will give me time to work on you.'

She bent her head to one side, studying him thoughtfully. He was up to something, and she couldn't for the moment figure out what it was. Nor did she have time to quiz him because Gemma came back just then, bringing Nicola over to the desk to meet up with James.

'Gemma, it's good to see you,' he said. Then, glancing down at Nicola, he added, 'How are you, angel? I heard that you fell on your arm.'

Nicola nodded. 'I was trying to skate round and round, but somebody banged into me and I fell over.'

'Oh, dear. Could I have a look at your arm, to see what you've done?'

'Yes, but don't pull it 'cos it hurts.'

'I won't, I promise.'

'Let's go through to the treatment room and I'll take a look at the films,' Louise suggested. 'You might want to glance at them too,' she suggested to James, 'and then you can let me know if you come to the same conclusion as me.'

A few minutes later, James finished studying the ultrasound scans and gave his verdict. 'I agree with you, there's a slight displacement of the medial epicondyle.' He glanced at Louise. 'What do you propose to do?'

'We'll treat it initially with an elbow splint.' She explained the process to Gemma. 'She'll wear the splint for about five days, and then we'll replace it with a sling. If she's making a good enough recovery by then, she might start to use the elbow as she feels able. It will probably be about four weeks before the injury is properly healed, and in the meantime I'll give her anti-inflammatory pain medication. We'll do a follow-up X-ray to make sure everything's as it should be.'

'Thanks,' Gemma said. 'You've been really good with her. It's a relief to know that nothing is fractured.'

Louise put the splint in place, and checked to make sure that the child was comfortable and relatively free from pain.

'It feels all right,' Nicola said. 'Thank you.'

'You're welcome, poppet.'

Gemma stood up, preparing to leave. 'We'd better go and fetch Anne-Marie,' she told Nicola. 'She'll be wondering what's happening.' Glancing at Louise, she said, 'James tells me that we'll be seeing you up at the house on Saturday. I'm glad about that. If you like, I'll show you around the studio where I do my painting from time to time.'

Louise gave her a smile. 'I'd enjoy that very much, thanks.'

James readied himself to leave with his sister and Nicola. 'I have to go back to my meeting,' he told Louise as they all moved out into the corridor. 'The committee is preparing for a public meeting where all the issues around the proposed closure can be aired.'

Her mouth made a straight line. 'I'd hoped that if you worked with us for a while you would soon begin to see where you were going wrong on that score.'

She watched as Gemma continued to make her way towards the main exit. 'I suppose, deep down, I was hoping that you would put your weight behind our arguments and try to sway the board in our favour. Some of those children who were involved in the traffic accident the other day might not have survived if the decision had been made to take them to the Royal Forest Hospital initially. Can't you see how important it is that we stay open?'

He lifted his arms to her, cupping her shoulders lightly with his palms and drawing her near to him. 'I'm sorry, Louise. I know how much this means to you, but we have to think of the wider picture. Your patients were fortunate in that they had a paramedic with them from the outset and that you were skilful enough and had the expertise to bring them back from the brink. I doubt they would have survived if a less skilled doctor had been in charge.'

'You don't know that.'

'I do. I've seen enough to know that you're the best there is, and to realise that we need you on our team at the Royal Forest Hospital. Would you think about it?'

She shook her head. 'No, I can't. This is where I need to be. I know that what you're planning to do is wrong, and that because of it patients will die. How can I persuade you to listen to me and take on board what I'm saying?'

Slowly, he drew her even closer to him, and in the next moment she heard him sigh and thought she felt the soft brush of his lips on her forehead. 'I am listening to you,' he said evenly. 'I'm not the enemy, Louise. I wish you would realise that. I just happen to think that you are blinded to everything by your love of this place.'

Then, as quickly as it had started, he let her go, and she began to wonder if she had imagined that kiss. She felt the imprint of it on her brow, as though he had seared her with his touch, but now he was walking away from her, heading towards the car park where his sister was waiting for him.

Louise stayed where she was for a while, struggling to get herself back together again. Why did she feel this way, torn between what she knew was right, and the gentle tug of her senses that told her she wanted to be with him, folded in his arms so that the rest of the world would retreat and dissolve into nothingness? That would surely be folly.

Saturday was a glorious reminder of what summer was all about. The sun was a bright golden orb in a spectacularly blue sky, and all around nature was burgeoning with fresh colour. Louise drank it all in as she drove to Ashleigh Manor, and tried to tell herself that this afternoon's gathering would be a time for her to unwind and enjoy the beautiful surroundings of a country manor.

There was no question of her not fitting in, was there? After all, she had an invitation, straight from James's own mouth, which had been followed up by the arrival on her doormat of a genteel gold-edged card, signed by Joseph.

So why was she feeling so unsure of herself?

James met her at the front of the house. 'I'm glad you came,' he said, looking her over as though to make sure she was truly here. Had he sensed her doubts?

'You look lovely,' he murmured in a husky tone, and she responded by absently smoothing down the folds of her dress. She had chosen to wear this particular one because the softly draping material flowed easily around her limbs as she walked, and the delicate flower pattern made her feel cheerful.

'Thank you.'

'Come and say hello to my grandfather. He's out in the garden, talking to Gemma.'

He led the way, his arm going lightly around her shoulders in a gesture that said she belonged, that she was part of their group and he was glad to have her here.

'Louise, my dear, we're just enjoying a fruit punch out here.' Joseph was sitting by a table that was set out on the terrace in front of open French windows that led into the sitting room, and now he beckoned her over to him. 'Let me pour you a glass.'

He reached out a shaky hand to the jug of iced juice, and James intervened. 'I'll do it,' he said. 'You sit back and rest.'

Louise was shocked by the old man's condition. He was even more frail than usual, his cheeks pale and his eyes had a weary look about them.

'Thank you, James.' Joseph patted the chair beside him. 'Come and sit down, Louise. Gemma has just gone to check on the children in the arbour. She worries about Nicola's arm, but my great-granddaughter is quite oblivious to any problems. She seems to be recovering nicely, thanks to you.'

'I expect she'll be fine,' Louise answered. 'I wanted

to tell you that I have the painting that you gave me in pride of place in my living room. It looks beautiful in there, and I'm so pleased to have it.'

He nodded, but then he frowned, putting a hand to his head momentarily.

'Are you all right?' James asked, a look of concern coming over his face.

'Yes, of course. It's nothing.' He rested his hand in his lap and looked at James. 'Would you tell Catherine that we're ready to eat?'

'I will.'

For the next hour they enjoyed a wonderful meal outside in the fresh air. Gemma told Louise about the landscape she was painting—a view of a lake from the vantage point of a hillside not too far away. Robert came to join them and talked about the new foal taking its first faltering steps around the paddock, and James came and sat next to her, making her smile with his accounts of his childhood at the Manor House.

'We had an argument with my father one day over who had been digging up plants in the kitchen garden. We were only small children at the time, and all three of us were guilty of trampling over the newly planted seed-beds and tugging at the lettuce leaves that were beginning to sprout. Then he asked us who had been stripping the raspberry canes of their fruit and we all denied it. Of course we didn't realise that our faces and hands were smeared with juice, and that there were lettuce leaves sticking out from the soil under our shoes.'

'Oh, dear.' Louise chuckled. 'What happened? Were you banished from the garden after that?'

He shook his head. 'He told us that we would have to spend time with the gardener and see how he worked there. It was actually a joy for us to do that. We all had a great time, learning how to plant vegetables and prune fruit stems, and I think that's where Robert gained his love of farming.'

He glanced at his brother for confirmation and Robert nodded. 'It didn't occur to me back then that I would one day be managing the whole lot. I exchanged vegetable growing for crops, fruit farming and forestry.'

'I don't have any such tales to tell,' she admitted. 'Most of my foster parents had pocket handkerchief-sized gardens, and a good portion of those were taken up with lawn. I did help out with the garden at the children's home occasionally, though. Mostly I liked to work in the greenhouse, pricking out the seedlings or potting flowering plants—very simple activities compared with what you have to do.'

She turned to Joseph to ask if he had strong opinions on how the land was farmed, but he was resting, leaning back in his chair with his eyes closed and a line etched into his brow. He hadn't touched any of the food.

'I think my grandfather has a headache,' James said. 'I'll go and fetch some painkillers for him from the house.'

'I'll show you my studio, if you like,' Gemma said, glancing at Louise. 'It was converted from one of the old barns near to where I have my house in the grounds.

We get the sun in there for a good many hours of the day, and it makes the lighting perfect. My husband likes to sit in there and just take in the atmosphere.'

'Sounds good to me.' Louise stood up and followed where Gemma led, casting a quick glance in James's direction. He looked worried, and she wondered if he thought his grandfather might be heading for a collapse.

Gemma's studio was exactly as she'd said it would be, a large room filled with light, where conditions were just right for painting. Canvases were set out against the walls or on easels, wonderful splashes of colour that looked intensely busy close up and yet from a distance a splendid panorama opened up to delight the connoisseur. She was a truly magnificent artist.

'Your work takes my breath away,' Louise told her, gazing around. 'These are all so carefully done, and I can just picture myself standing in some of these woodland glades. The tree bark is so lifelike that it makes me want to reach out and touch it.'

Gemma laughed. 'Feel free. I do like working in oils. There's such a depth to the images you can create, but equally I like the softer look of watercolours.'

They spent some time looking at the canvases, until Anne-Marie came to find her mother and drag her back to the house.

'I want you to show me how to set up the wooden village toys and the railway track,' she said. 'Nicola keeps trying but she can only use one hand and she keeps knocking things over. Uncle Robert's too busy and he's gone off to see what's going on in the hen house. He says that so-and-so fox is sniffing about and if he catches him he'll take a shot at him.'

Gemma stifled a chuckle. 'Oh, dear, that's not good, is it? What about your Uncle James? He usually helps out with these things, doesn't he?'

Anne-Marie put on a serious face. 'He says Grandad is feeling poorly and he thought me and Nicola should go and play in the summerhouse. I told him I'd help him to look after Grandad but he said no, he would do it by himself.' She was thoughtful for a moment. 'I think he wanted to be left on his own.' Then she looked at her mother. 'Why would he want us to go away? We weren't being naughty.'

Gemma frowned. 'I don't know, Anne-Marie. Perhaps Grandad needed to be quiet for a while.'

Anne-Marie seemed to accept that well enough, and they all left the studio shortly after that, with Gemma heading for the summerhouse and telling Louise, 'I'll come and join you on the terrace in a minute or two.'

'That's all right. I'll see if James needs a helping hand.'

James, though, didn't respond to Louise's offer of help when she arrived back at the terrace. He didn't acknowledge her in any way, but simply sat in the chair by his grandfather's side, staring straight ahead.

'James, what's wrong?'

He didn't answer and then, as she sent a quick glance towards Joseph, she could see why he was acting in such a strange manner. 'Oh, no,' she said in a broken voice. 'Oh, James, I'm so sorry. What happened? He seemed fine most of the afternoon.'

'I think it was a stroke,' James said at last. 'He died in my arms just a few minutes ago, but I don't think he was aware of what was happening. It was so quick…and so final. A whole lifetime of endeavour and experience wiped out in a matter of seconds.'

She knelt down in front of him, clasping his hands in her own. 'I'm so, so sorry. Is there anything I can do?'

He shook his head and didn't even look at her. 'I just need to be on my own for a while.'

'Yes…yes, of course.' Somehow, she hadn't been expecting that, and she struggled to take in the fact that he didn't want her around.

Logic told her that of course he wanted to be left alone to take in this awful event, but her instincts warned her that he was pushing her away in his hour of need, and that was no easy thing for her to accept.

'I'll leave you be, then,' she said in a husky tone. 'Perhaps it would be best if I go and watch over the children for a while, so that you can all take this in.'

He didn't answer her and she got to her feet, glancing once more at Joseph, who was at peace now, with a gentle smile frozen on his lips. An unbearable feeling of sadness washed over her.

CHAPTER NINE

'I THOUGHT James was looking particularly subdued this morning,' Jenny murmured. She carefully adjusted the amount of fluid that was to be infused into her small patient, while Louise checked the dressing on the three-year-old girl's chest. The child's skin was reddened from a nasty scald. 'In fact, I'm surprised that he has been able to come in to work at all over these last few weeks, because I know how sad he was over his grandfather's passing…and I imagine he's had a lot to do, with putting his grandfather's affairs in order.'

'Yes, I noticed that he was a lot quieter than usual today,' Louise agreed in a quiet tone, 'but when I tried to get to the bottom of things, he said he had to go over to the resuscitation bay and didn't have time to talk. As to coming in to work, I know that he doesn't want to take any more time off than is necessary.'

She put the last tape in place around the dressing. 'I offered him the chance to take an extended leave, but he turned me down. Once the funeral was over, he made up his mind that he wanted to keep busy, and he said that coming in to work would help to keep him focused.'

She looked down at the child she was tending. 'Does that feel more comfortable, sweetheart?' she asked her and, when the toddler nodded, she said with a smile, 'That's good. You're doing very well.'

She went to search in a nearby cupboard, and came back to the bedside holding a teddy bear. 'Would you like to have him next to you in bed?' she asked. 'I think teddy hurts too, and I expect he needs a cuddle.'

The girl nodded and held out her hands to the silky bear, a smile hovering on her mouth.

The child's mother gave a relieved sigh as the little girl settled back against her pillows, winding a protective arm around the bear, her fingers stroking his soft fur. 'Will the skin heal without any scarring?' the mother asked, looking anxiously at Louise.

Louise nodded. 'Hopefully, there won't be any permanent damage, although it will take around three weeks for the skin to repair itself. This is a second-degree burn, and the dressings will help her to heal. With any luck she won't need to be on the drip for too long. In the meantime, I'll arrange for her to be admitted so that we can keep an eye on her for the next day or so.'

Coming away from the observation ward a few minutes later, she waited for Jenny to catch up with her.

'It must be very difficult for James right now,' the nurse chatted on. 'His whole world must have changed with his grandfather's passing. He has to take over the running of Ashleigh Manor, and after the meeting with the solicitor the other day his family must be wondering how they are going to go on. I heard his sister telling you about it. The reading of the will must have come as a shock to all of them.'

'Yes, I think it did.' Louise pressed her lips together, remembering how Gemma had responded to the details contained in the will. She had brought Nicola to the hospital for her follow-up examination, and had confided her news to Louise. 'James has been very tight lipped about everything. I think they had expected to have free rein with the running of the place, but it turned out that a lot of the money that had been put in trust for them was tied up with conditions.'

She added her signature to the girl's chart and placed it down on the desk. 'I would have thought there was some way they could get around the restrictions, but apparently not. Their grandfather wanted to keep the property sacrosanct, and had the lawyers draw everything up tight as a drum. Of course, he didn't appear to take into account the impact that death duties would have on the estate.'

'What will they do? I don't suppose James and his sister will be too concerned, but his brother was never very happy with the situation, was he?'

'No, he wasn't. Robert wanted to run things his own way.'

Louise glanced at her watch and saw that it was close to lunch time. Things had been so busy around the unit up to now that she hadn't even found time for a morning coffee break. 'I think I might grab a takeaway lunch from the staff restaurant and head over to the park for a while,' she said. 'Tim will be on hand here if anything crops up, but you can page me if there are any problems.'

Jenny nodded. 'Okay.'

Louise started for the exit, coming across James as he left one of the treatment rooms and was beginning to make his way towards the locker room. 'Are you going off for your lunch break?' she asked him.

'Yes. I thought I would take it now while things are relatively quiet.' He studied her thoughtfully. 'Why? Is there a problem? Do you need me to stay?'

She shook her head. 'No, but I wanted to warn you that the press are out in force at the front of the building again.' She made a rueful face. 'I organised a survey amongst people who used the A&E department and a lot of the parents of children who were treated here have decided to get involved with our cause. So you might want to use a different exit.' She smiled gently. 'I don't think you're in any mood to deal with them right now, are you?'

'That's true. I'm not,' he acknowledged, giving her a brief narrowed glance, noting that she was wearing a light jacket over her skirt and top. 'Are you going out?'

'Yes, I thought I would go and eat my lunch in the park. Would you like to join me? We could probably both do with getting away from here for a while, and it's a bright day out there. It seems a shame to miss out on the sunshine.'

He hesitated for a moment, and then nodded. 'That sounds like a good idea. We could escape through the back exit, couldn't we?'

They stopped off at the staff restaurant to pick up some food for lunch, and then walked towards the nearby park.

'I sometimes come out here and eat my sandwiches at a bench table overlooking the lake,' she told him. 'I find it really peaceful, and there's a lovely sunny spot close to the pavilion. It helps me to unwind, looking out over the surface of the water and watching the wildfowl dart among the reeds, especially if I've had a particularly bad morning.'

James scanned the landscaped gardens as they walked through the park gates. 'My grandfather loved this place,' he said. 'I think he told you that when you first met him in here. Like you, he enjoyed the tranquillity, and when he was younger he would come here to think things through whenever he had a problem he needed to solve. I suppose he had so many things on his mind, things he never talked about to us, but as head of the Ashleigh estate he must have had a great many concerns to occupy his thoughts.'

'He probably found that if he stayed on the estate he would become sidetracked. Sometimes it's better to get right away and look at things from a different perspective.' Louise pointed out a bench seat in the distance. 'We can sit over there, if you like,' she murmured. 'There's no one else around, so we won't be disturbed.'

'Okay.' They crossed the sweeping meadow grass

and laid their packages out on the rustic wooden table. Between them, they had a variety of crisp bread rolls and ready prepared dishes of salad, along with a mayonnaise dip. Louise had bought a bowl of fresh fruit salad for dessert, and they both had bottled drinks to wash it all down.

She sat down opposite James and sent him a surreptitious glance. 'I imagine that you were surprised when your grandfather insisted on maintaining his control over the property even after he had passed on.'

She helped herself to lettuce and sliced tomato. 'Gemma explained how he was determined to keep visitors from invading the property. She said it was one of the ideas that Robert had in mind for increasing the revenue of the estate, and now his plans have been dashed. What do you think about it? Has it caused a lot of trouble for you?'

James broke off some of his bread and savoured it, along with a round soft cheese. 'It isn't a problem for me particularly, in as much as I tended to agree with my grandfather. Ashleigh Manor is our home, and I didn't particularly want to see it opened up to the public. Robert, on the other hand, is always looking to the future, and he was hoping that one day he might put some of his ideas into practice. The will came as something of a blow to him, because now he feels that his hands are tied.'

Louise grimaced. 'I'm sure that your grandfather was doing his best for all of you. He was such a thoughtful, kind man, and he must have felt his obligations very strongly. I was surprised when he gave me the picture of my house, and I was afraid that he might have been acting on a whim. But when I got to know him better, I realised that he gave everything deep consideration and he was very sincere in everything that he did.'

'Yes, that's true. The sad thing is, we all loved our grandfather very much, and he was only doing what he thought was best to ensure the future for all of us. We know why he did what he did, and mostly we can appreciate it, but for Robert it has been almost too much for him to handle.'

She sent him a quick look, sensing that there was more that he was not telling her. 'Has something happened?'

He nodded. 'Robert walked out over the weekend. He said that he'd had enough, that it was a constant struggle for no real gain, and he had to go away and spend some time on his own. He packed a case and drove off without telling us where he was going.'

Louise gave a small gasp. 'Do you think he will be in touch some time soon? Surely he can't mean to stay away for very long?'

James lifted his shoulders briefly. 'I've no way of knowing. He's been gone for a couple of days already. I've been trying to call him, but he must have switched off his mobile phone.' He winced. 'I just wish that he had stayed long enough for us to talk things through. We would have come up with a solution between us, I'm sure.'

She reached out and lightly touched his hand in a

sympathetic gesture. It was a brief contact, but she wanted, more than anything, to show him how much she cared, and when he squeezed her fingers gently in return she was content. 'You'll be able to track him down eventually, though, won't you? If the police were to look for him, they would know if he uses his credit card, and then he could probably be traced.'

'I'm not sure they would do that if he left of his own free will. There's nothing to say that a person can't do that.'

'But you're not just an ordinary member of the public, are you? If you wanted to, you could pull strings, couldn't you?'

'Possibly. But I don't think I would want to use my position in that way, unless it was very necessary.'

She looked at him, her green eyes full of concern. 'What will you do? Is there someone you can rely on who will take over the running of the farm and the land in the meantime?'

'I'll do it myself. It's my job, as head of the family.'

Louise pulled in a quick breath. 'How will you be able to do that with all your other commitments?' She frowned. 'Do you need me to release you from your contract?'

He shook his head. 'That would leave you in the lurch, wouldn't it? I wouldn't do that.'

She swallowed some of her cold drink. 'Have you thought this through properly? It isn't just an ordinary household that you're running, is it? The Ashleigh estate is a huge business enterprise, and it seems to me that you've always tried to avoid getting too deeply involved with it. In fact, I'm surprised that Robert kept it going as well as he did, and perhaps it wasn't as easy as it looked. After all, there must have been a reason why he wanted to change things.'

'I may have avoided it, but I've always been conscious of my responsibilities in that direction.' He made a grimace. 'That's why I kept a weather eye on things to make sure that it was going smoothly, so I know what needs to be done. I just didn't want Robert to feel that he was being monitored in any way, so I stayed in the background.'

She looked at him with renewed respect. So he hadn't opted out entirely.

He helped himself to crunchy salad leaves and then added, 'I think Robert always felt that there was so much more potential locked up in the estate. It wasn't enough for him to manage the land and bring in enough income to keep the status quo. The upkeep of a place like Ashleigh Manor can be horrendous, and there's always the possibility that we would be faced with huge bills for repairs.'

He grimaced. 'In fact, the roof over my grandfather's area of the house is beginning to show signs of wear and tear. My grandfather knew about it, and it's something that we're going to have to address very soon. That's why we need to make the estate work for us. Robert wanted to build on what we have, and he believed that if we were to open up the house to visitors we could broaden our investments.'

'Have they been hit hard now that your grandfather has gone? Gemma said that the death duties were a big problem.'

'They are, but only inasmuch as my grandfather wanted to make an ongoing commitment to the fund for the running of the paediatric A&E unit at the Royal Forest Hospital. That may not be possible in the future. I need to work on that and see if I can come up with something that will enable us to carry out his wishes. I wouldn't want to see my grandfather's dreams abandoned. It was important to him to go on with the funding.'

Louise was silent for a while, thinking about that. From her point of view, the unit at the Royal Forest Hospital was in direct competition with her own, but it was something that Joseph had particularly cared about, and she could understand why his grandson would want to go on with what he had started.

'There's a lot that you need to think about, isn't there?' she murmured. 'I hope that Robert comes to his senses and you'll be able to work together on this.'

'So do I.' He cast a glance over the empty cartons and packages that were strewn about the table. 'Have you had enough to eat? There are still some cracker biscuits and a couple of small cheeses if you'd like them.'

'No, thank you. I'm full up.' She made a negative gesture with her hands to emphasise the point. 'I suppose we should make a start on clearing up. It's almost time for us to be going back to the hospital.'

He cleared away the debris of their meal, throwing the wrappings and containers into a bin that was close by, and a short time later they began to walk back across the park, taking a slightly different route through the shrub garden.

They passed by the Pets' Corner, hidden away in a shady area, and Louise stopped for a moment to look at the animals.

'Joseph asked me if there was an aviary here, and I said there were rabbits and guinea pigs, but no birds as far as I knew—I remember he said that things change—but look, there is an aviary, after all.' She pointed to a large structure that was fronted by meshed wire. Brightly coloured budgerigars and canaries flitted from branch to branch, the noise of their chirruping filling the air, and in a separate section parakeets preened themselves. Her expression was sad. 'I wish he had been able to come and see it.'

James put an arm around her. 'You miss him too, don't you?'

'I do. Especially being here, in the park…it brings it all back to me. I just remember him so vividly, and how sweet he was, even though he was ill.' Her voice became muffled, and James gave her a squeeze.

'He was very fond of you. He was glad that you and I were working together. He said that we could learn from one another, but I've no idea what he meant by that.' He smiled down at her, and it was all Louise could do not to cry. She felt the tears pricking at her eyelids, and she blinked, trying to dash them away.

'I'm sorry,' she said. 'I don't know why I'm be-having like this. You're the one who has suffered a dreadful loss, but I just feel so sad that he's gone.'

James curled up his hand and gently rested it beneath her chin, tilting her face up to him. 'It's all right to feel that way,' he said softly. 'It's good that we all mourn him. He was an exceptional man.'

She nodded and, before she could stop them, salt tears trickled down her cheeks. James held her close, sharing her sorrow, his head bent close to hers, his cheek resting against her cheek.

Then she gave a ragged sigh, looking up at him, and in that instant his head lowered slowly, coming closer and closer until his lips were touching hers, brushing against them, testing their soft fullness. Then he laid claim to her mouth, totally, in a fierce, passionate kiss.

A swift, hot surge of need rippled through her body like a forest fire, consuming everything in its path. The kiss was everything she wanted, needed, hoped for, taking her breath away and devouring her in its inten-sity. Her lips parted beneath his, absorbing his passion and desire, making her desperate in that moment to be one with him.

Obligingly, his arms went around her, holding her tight, and he moved her into the shelter of the shrub-bery so that they were hidden from sight, away from the prying eyes of anyone who might happen to pass by. The softness of her curves was crushed against his long body, her legs pressured by the taut, muscled strength of his thighs.

'I've waited so long to hold you this way,' he said, his voice roughened, his breath escaping him in uneven bursts. 'I wanted to kiss you, to take you into my arms and feel the warmth of your body next to mine.'

His hands travelled over her, sliding beneath her jacket, tracing the contours of her feminine shape. 'You are so lovely, Louise…my Louise…why have I waited for you for so long?'

She gazed up at him, her mind hazy with yearning. Was he really saying these wonderful words to her…or was she so taken up with the enchantment of the moment that she had imagined it?

Her hand slid down over the smooth wall of his chest. This was real enough, though, and she could feel the beat of his heart beneath her fingertips, a heavy, discordant thud that told her he was every bit as overwhelmed as she was.

Then something began to intrude on her senses, breaking the spell. From a distance, there came the sound of voices, the light tread of people approaching along the nearby path, and Louise became very still, struggling to pull herself together.

What was she doing, kissing him in a public park, allowing her wayward senses to drive everything out of her mind but the need to have him hold her?

Perhaps James was thinking along much the same lines because he reluctantly eased himself away from her, steadying her with his hands as though he feared she might lose her balance.

And so she might, because the enormity of what had

happened suddenly swept over her. She had lost all thought of time and place, had wanted him in those breathless moments to the exclusion of all else, and now she realised with sudden shock that there could only be one possible explanation for that.

She had fallen in love with him. Against all the odds, despite the fact that he had the power to destroy everything she had worked for, she loved him. It was madness, a wild, reckless emotion, because nothing could ever come of it.

His world was light years away from hers. His titled family had moved through generation after generation amongst the rich and famous. His grandfather had endowed the Royal Forest Hospital with a precious gift that threatened to destroy her own dream, and James would not do anything to save what she had built up. Her love for him was doomed from the outset.

'Perhaps we should go,' he said in an even tone, bringing her back to cold, harsh reality. 'We'll be needed back at the hospital.'

She nodded, not trusting herself to speak just then, and he led the way, his stride as purposeful as ever.

Both of their lives had changed in different ways in these last few weeks, but he would work steadfastly to conquer his demons. She didn't think she would ever come to terms with hers.

CHAPTER TEN

'THE child's lung has collapsed. Jenny, I'll give her intravenous analgesia and lidocaine, but I need to put a chest tube in place—quickly.' Louise worked swiftly to identify the point of incision, but looked up momentarily from the patient she was tending to see that Alice had hurried into the room.

'Is something wrong, Alice?'

'Yes. James's patient is struggling to breathe and needs to go to Theatre right now. There's no anaesthetist available and all the Theatres are occupied. He said to tell you that he's taking him up to the endoscopy suite.'

Louise frowned, carefully infiltrating lidocaine beneath the child's skin. 'All the surgeons are involved with patients right now—and being the weekend we're short staffed. It will be at least an hour before we could expect Mr Morrison to get here. Our Senior House Officers and the registrar are all working on the trauma victims who came in earlier.'

'That's what I told him but he says it's not a problem.

He'll do the procedure himself, but we need to transfer the boy for endoscopy right now. His condition is deteriorating with every moment.'

'You'd better go and assist, then,' Louise told her, getting ready to make the incision in her patient's chest. 'I'll come and find you as soon as I'm finished here.'

'All right. I'll tell him.'

Louise watched as Alice went out of the room. Through the glass panel that divided one treatment room from another, she saw that James was setting up an intravenous line in the little boy's arm, and all around him monitors were bleeping warnings at regular intervals.

Louise inserted the chest tube and connected it to an underwater seal. Then she sutured the drain in place and covered it with a dressing and adhesive tape.

'That seems to be working just fine,' she told Jenny a moment or two later. 'Her breathing is becoming easier, but I'll need an X-ray of her chest to confirm that the tube hasn't been inserted too far. Page me if there's a problem, will you? I'll be in the endoscopy suite.'

'I'll see to it.' Jenny went to check on the little girl, and Louise left the treatment room and headed for the corridor.

She caught up with James and Alice as they were about to enter the lift. 'What do we have?' she asked quietly, stepping inside with them. She looked down at the boy, a five-year-old who was feverish and breathing rapidly, in clear distress. Each breath he pulled in was accompanied by a high-pitched sound that denoted a blockage somewhere in his respiratory system.

James checked the boy's intravenous line and then adjusted the face mask, making sure that the child was receiving an adequate supply of oxygen.

'I think it's a bacterial tracheitis,' James explained, using a low tone so as not to disturb the child. He punched the button and the lift started to move. 'His throat's closing up because of the swelling and I need to get a tube in there before his oxygen saturation level falls any lower. We're running out of time. He's been feverish over the last few days, according to the parents, with a barking cough and runny nose. He complained of a sore throat and his voice is hoarse. I've examined him, and the lung sounds are decreased in the right lower lobe, with fine crackles.'

'So you're going to intubate him and take a look at what's going on?'

James nodded and, as the lift doors opened on the next floor, he started to wheel the boy towards the endoscopy suite. There was urgency in his movements and Louise could see why he was so worried. The boy was in greater danger of asphyxiation with every moment that passed.

'I'm going to anaesthetise him through a breathing mask,' James told Louise as they settled the child in the room. 'He's not in any state to worry about what's going on, and it will be easier for him that way.'

'All right. I'll act as your anaesthetist, and you can do the procedures.' She glanced at Alice. 'Do we have a consent form from the parents?'

Alice nodded. 'The duty nurse is explaining things to them.'

'That's good. Will you assist with preparing samples for the lab?'

'Yes, of course.'

Just a couple of minutes later, the boy was anaesthetised and James was ready to insert a five millimetre endotracheal tube into the child's throat.

Louise set about collecting blood samples and passed on the vials to Alice for marking up. 'We need a complete blood count and cultures,' she told her.

James, in the meantime, had started on the various diagnostic examinations, using a laryngoscope first of all. 'The vocal cords are swollen,' he said, his voice showing his concern, and then he moved quickly on to perform a tracheoscopy.

He winced. 'The trachea is coated with purulent secretions and the mucosa is ulcerated, with sloughing into the tracheal lumen. I'll do what I can to remove the secretions with suction, and you can prepare the samples for testing, Alice. We'll need them checked for Gram stain, culture and sensitivities to antibiotic therapy.'

He worked for a few minutes until he was satisfied that he had cleared as much as he could. Then he went on to check the boy's lung. 'There are the same secretions here,' he said. 'I'll do what I can to remove them.'

'From the looks of things he'll need strong intravenous antibiotic cover,' Louise said. 'Do you want me to start that for you?'

James nodded. 'Yes. Give him cefuroxime to begin

with. He's already had broad-spectrum penicillin, but if it's a staph aureus infection, as I suspect, the cefuroxime should help to combat it. I can only hope that the secretions don't start to build up again too quickly.'

'Okay.' Louise began to prepare the medication. 'What are you going to do about the endotracheal tube?'

'I'll replace it with a nasotracheal one as soon as I've finished, and we'll keep him on positive pressure ventilation. At least his breathing has improved a little already.'

James glanced at the video monitor a few minutes later. 'I think I've done about all I can here. We'd better transfer him to intensive care, and let the parents know what's happening.'

Louise smiled at him. 'You did a great job.' Glancing at Alice, she added, 'You too, Alice. Thanks for everything.'

Alice nodded. 'I just hope the little chap recovers fast. I'll never get used to seeing them like this, so ill and helpless. That was such a close thing. It's alarming.' She sighed. 'To be honest, I sometimes wonder why I do this job…it can be so distressing.'

'But then they start feeling better and begin to demand attention, and you know exactly why you do it.' Louise said, her mouth curving. 'Let's get this little one off to ICU, shall we?'

She knew exactly what Alice was feeling, though. It was something they all went through, and the sad fact was that working with children could be heart-breaking at times.

She wrote up the forms for the laboratory tests and handed them to Alice. 'I'd better get back to my trauma patients,' she murmured.

It was some time later, when she was taking a break outside in the quadrangle at the back of the A&E unit, that James came to join her.

'So this is where you've been hiding,' he said softly, walking over to her in the far corner of the paved square. A patch of lawn edged the terrace and trees grew at intervals, providing shade. 'Alice said you might be here, but I almost missed you, out of sight here behind the cherry tree.'

'It makes a good refuge, and it's peaceful,' Louise murmured. 'I'm surprised you haven't discovered this place for yourself before now.'

'I can see why you like it,' he said, coming to sit down beside her on the wooden bench. 'I thought you'd like to know that I've just finished speaking to the boy's parents and they're going to stay with him in the inten-sive care unit. It'll be a while before we know if he's going to be all right, but we've done all we can for now.'

'Those sorts of cases are always scary, aren't they—when the child can't breathe and the swelling is blocking the windpipe?'

He nodded. 'As you said to Alice, that's when you realise why you came into medicine in the first place, because you know you can make a difference. These last few weeks have certainly made me think again about why I wanted to become a doctor. I think, over the years, I had begun to lose sight of that.'

He sent her a thoughtful look. 'You know, it occurred to me, back in the endoscopy suite, that while we were going through all that worry, feeling the urgency of the situation, you had the opportunity, but you never once stated the obvious.'

'What would that be?' She returned his gaze, noting the way his mouth slanted in wry amusement, and her green eyes shimmered because after all the drama of the day he was a sight for sore eyes and she was glad he was here beside her.

'That he wouldn't have made it if he'd had to go all the way to the Royal Forest Hospital.'

'Ah, yes, he wouldn't have stood a chance, would he?' She made a brief grimace. 'Well…I thought maybe it was best if you came to that conclusion all by yourself. I knew you would manage it, given time.'

She laughed softly, relieved that he should finally come to realise the truth of what she was saying. She couldn't help wondering, though, whether it would make any difference at all. Wasn't the board of Trustees holding a public meeting this very week, to promote its plan for a super, winner takes all, hospital? 'Not that it matters now. The Trust won't be changing its mind any time soon, will it, despite all the action we've taken to try to persuade them otherwise?'

'Well, maybe, maybe not. If you want to have any chance of swaying the board, you'll need to come up with reasons why they need your unit to be here, and how any measures you put in place will be cost-effective.'

Her brows lifted. 'So it's about saving money, after all?'

'Not necessarily. But they'll be more likely to listen if you have some ideas about reducing costs.'

'How about a mention of all the video conferencing facilities that are in place here already? Why travel to the Royal Forest Hospital when people are on hand here who can carry out intricate procedures and who can advise doctors in hospitals all around via the video link? How about the fact that we have an untapped source of GPs locally who have expressed a willingness to use our outpatient facilities to treat both adult and paediatric patients during weekend hours?'

'They have?' He lifted a dark brow.

'Oh, yes, but only because they have the opportunity to transfer seriously ill patients to our units and they know they can rely on the support of our specialist staff. They won't be able to do that if the A&E is closed down, because other wards and facilities will go along with us. We've been learning how to work together to bring about these extra services, but that will all be wasted in the end, won't it?'

She was itemising the points in her head and now she went on, 'Added to that, we've developed treatment regimes that lead to shorter hospital stays without detriment to the patient. We've also reduced waiting times, so we get to treat more patients.'

She looked at him. 'These are all proven ways of reducing costs, according to the mantra of hospital managers. Would you like me to go on? It always seems an odd sort of way of balancing the books to me— saving money by seeing more patients, but then I'm not an economist. To me it's all a pointless exercise in shifting statistics from one page to another.'

He chuckled. 'No, there's no need for you to add any more. I think you've proved your point well enough. What I suggest is that you put it in writing and present it to the board, along with case studies of the patients who wouldn't have made it if they'd had to travel to the Royal Forest. Add to that the backing of parents whose children were treated here, and you might make some headway.'

She sat back and simply stared at him. 'I'm amazed,' she murmured. 'I didn't think I would see the day when you would be prepared to support me in this.'

'Don't get too carried away,' he told her. 'I'm on the Trust board and I know how these people think. It isn't at all cut and dried.'

She sobered. 'Yes, I suppose that's true.' Her joy was short lived. 'And you have problems of your own to contend with, don't you? Has Robert still not come home?'

He shook his head. 'I haven't been able to get in touch with him. He's still not answering any calls.'

She frowned. 'You could always send him a text message. Let him know of any ideas you might come up with for getting the most out of the estate. I know he was concerned about the terms of your grandfather's will—are you still struggling with that?'

'It has certainly concentrated my mind these last

few weeks. I'm head of the estate now, but I was hoping that I would be able to keep Robert on board. It would be good if I could find a way around the problems we're having and come up with ways to make the changes he wanted.'

Her mouth made a wry shape. 'Yes, I've been giving some thought to that.'

'You have?'

She nodded. 'From what you told me, and bits I've gleaned from Gemma, you can't open up the house for visitors on an everyday basis, but there's nothing to say that your grandfather would have objected to you allowing people to look round at certain times of the year, or on occasion by appointment.'

He wasn't making any attempt to interrupt, and so she went on. 'Then again, I imagine there might be television and film companies who would be glad of the opportunity to use the house occasionally as a background for period television and film productions. There's nothing in the will to say that you can't allow that, is there, and in one way your grandfather might have appreciated that, because it would showcase the house and allow it to be seen in its historical setting.'

His eyes widened a fraction and, since he hadn't dismissed the idea outright, she warmed to her theme. 'Then, of course, there are the grounds—nothing was laid down about them not being used for things like equestrian events, was there? Robert would probably be enthusiastic about building up the stables once more, and you could perhaps use them as a base for riding lessons. Your grandfather would probably have approved of that, especially if you were to have sessions for disabled children so that they could experience the thrill of the outdoors. And then there's the lake—I imagine people would jump at the chance to buy licenses to fish there. It's such a tranquil place.'

He smiled into her eyes and draped an arm lightly around her shoulders. 'You really have been thinking this through, haven't you?'

Her confidence grew under the gentle encouragement of his embrace. There was a warm familiarity about the way he was holding her, and she wanted nothing more than to snuggle up against him and have him show her that he cared for her every bit as much as she cared for him.

She wasn't at all sure about that, though. It was some time now since he had told her how much he wanted her and needed her, and how desperate he was to kiss her, and she had to accept that he had done it on the spur of the moment, and it didn't necessarily mean that he loved her in return, did it?

'I tried to think of things from your grandfather's point of view,' she explained. 'He was proud of his heritage, but he also wanted to keep the family together as a unit, living within the family home and appreciating it for its historic value. What he didn't want was its wholesale use as a marketing venture.'

'Yes, I think that's probably true. He was a very private man, but he was also very conscious of the history of the Manor and the estate.'

She hesitated. 'Perhaps that's what's behind Robert's mood. Maybe he wants to share his pride in the family's history with others, and in a way celebrate everything that the house and the estate represent. He's feeling thwarted and undervalued, and somehow you need to draw him back into the fold.'

James gave her a hug. 'It's very sweet of you to think about me and my family in this way. My grandfather thought you were great, and that's how I feel about you too.' His mouth softened in a smile. 'I wish I could show you how glad I am that you came into my life. You've given me a whole new perspective on things.'

'I have?' She gazed up at him, loving the way he folded her into the warmth of his body, and even as he nodded in response he was drawing her closer, his head lowering so that his lips touched hers, softening in a gentle kiss that made her whole body tingle with blissful pleasure.

She kissed him in return, her lips clinging to his, her mind reeling with a myriad of sensations that ran through her body as his hand lightly stroked the curve of her cheek and slid down to trace the silken column of her throat.

His touch was exquisite, bringing every nerve-ending to clamouring life, and making her long for more—she wanted to feel his hands moving over her in tender exploration, and for a moment she thought she must have spoken aloud because his hand trailed over her, sliding down towards the scooped neckline of her cotton top and lingering there.

Could he feel the heavy beat of her heart beneath his fingers? Surely he must, because it was pounding so hard that she could feel her breath constricting in her throat, and heat was spreading through her with all the intensity of a desert sunrise.

'You're the best thing that's happened to me in a long time,' he said, his tone roughened. 'I wish I could take you away from here and show you just how much I want you…' He broke off, a ragged sigh breaking in his throat. 'But I can't do that. It wouldn't be right.'

He leaned his forehead lightly against hers, murmuring softly against her temple. 'There are too many things getting in the way. Not the least of which is my position here at the hospital, and my dealings with the board of Trustees. And the problem of the Ashleigh estate.'

His hands cupped her arms and he held her away from him a fraction, reluctantly, as though he was battling with himself and wrestling with his conscience. 'I can't do this. And I know that you want to help, but I can sort out my own problems. I don't need you to think up ways to make things right. You have enough worries of your own right now, with the board meeting and the whole future of your department in jeopardy. Thanks for what you're trying to do, but I'll cope on my own.'

She stared at him in bewilderment. What had she done wrong? Why had he changed, all in a matter of minutes? One moment he'd been holding her and kissing her, making her feel warm and secure, and the next he had put her at a distance, as though nothing could ever come of their liaison.

What had brought about this change in him? Was he conscious of his allegiance to the Trust and all that entailed? Had he, too, realised how far apart they were in everything that they believed in?

He let her go and then stood up, looking down at her where she stayed, frozen like a statue on the bench. 'I have to go and check on my patients,' he said in a quiet tone. 'I realise now I should never have kissed you. I'm sorry.'

He walked away, and all she could think of was that her heart was thudding, a chaotic, overpowering beat, and her mind was dazed, incapable of taking in what he was saying to her.

He had kissed her and then left her, without even a backward glance. There would never be any future for them together, and it broke her heart.

CHAPTER ELEVEN

'HAVE you heard anything about how the Trust board meeting went the other day?' Jenny passed a patient's chart to Louise for signing, and Louise quickly glanced through the notes.

'Nothing, so far. It all seems to be very hush-hush. I think they're preparing a statement for the press and trying to arrange a public meeting so that they can air their recommendations.' Louise added her signature to the chart.

'Hasn't James said anything to you about it?'

She frowned. 'No, he's been very quiet on that score. I expect he's been sworn to secrecy until they make the public announcement.' She checked her list of patients and then went with the nurse in search of the accident victim who had just come back from the radiology department.

'You've broken a bone in your leg,' she told the ten-year-old boy when she had studied his X-ray films in the light box, 'but it's a clean break, and we'll be able to put your leg in a plaster cast to make sure that it heals properly. I'll make sure that you have plenty of pain medication, so that you shouldn't be too uncomfortable.' She left the boy in Jenny's care, and went to look at another patient.

Over the last couple of weeks, James seemed to have been in a perpetual rush, dividing his time between management meetings and his work in A&E and, she suspected, dealing with the overwhelming burden of managing the Ashleigh estate.

'I've arranged for someone to come and start on the roof repairs,' he had told her some time ago, 'but, before they can do anything, I have to make sure that all the attics are cleared. It's a marathon task because my grandfather seems to have sent everything up there for storage over the years.'

Lately, whenever she had come across him in the course of their work, he had been totally professional, but there had been no opportunity for them to talk in the way that she had become used to. His manner was faintly distracted and, although she could understand why that might be, it hurt to know that the intimacy that had grown between them had dissolved so abruptly.

She saw him now, walking across the central area, and for a moment or two she hesitated, wondering whether to take a few minutes to go and talk to him. Then she saw that Gemma had come into the waiting-room, and she guessed that he was on his way to meet her.

Gemma's art gallery wasn't too far distant from the hospital and it was fairly easy for her to come across here to see her brother from time to time. Louise saw them hug one another, and it was good to see the affection between them, but it only served to make her feel all the more isolated. She missed his warm embraces and his gentle smile.

He was frowning now, and Gemma was talking earnestly to him, while James shook his head every now and again. Gemma handed him some papers and he glanced briefly down at them before tucking them into his inside jacket pocket.

He smiled at his sister and kissed her lightly on the cheek, before moving briskly away. Louise saw him go into one of the treatment rooms.

'Hello, Gemma,' she said softly in greeting as Gemma passed on her way out. 'It's lovely to see you again. How are you and the girls? Are you all bearing up well enough these last few weeks?'

'Louise, it's good to see you.' Gemma's face lit up. 'I wondered if I might run into you while I was here. You and James are always so busy.'

'James has been certainly, these last few weeks. I expect he has a lot to do, sorting out the management of the estate.'

'I think he's worked out more or less what he wants to do regarding that. We just need to bring Robert back on board, but it's difficult, seeing that he won't answer our phone calls.'

'I'm sorry. I'd hoped he would be back with you by now.'

Gemma shook her head, her mouth making a rueful

shape. 'He's probably best out of it at the moment. The workmen are all over the house, fixing anything that needs to be fixed, and it's pretty chaotic. I'm acting as a go-between, which is why I've brought in a list of queries from the builders today. James is run ragged keeping on top of everything these days.'

Louise nodded. 'I guessed as much. He seems to have a lot on his mind of late, and it hasn't been easy to get him to stop and talk about anything. I had hoped he might give me some idea of what's going on with the plans for the hospital, but he's probably been asked to say nothing, and of course he has so much else going on right now.'

A small line indented Gemma's brow. 'I didn't think he would have said anything to you. He's always been that way, keeping things to himself and not wanting to confide in anyone. I've been telling him that he should share some of his problems, but he won't do it…even where the estate is concerned, he keeps it all to himself. It's very frustrating. He thinks he's being protective of us, shouldering the burden himself, but I just find it plain annoying.'

Louise smiled. 'I know the feeling.'

Gemma touched her arm in a gesture of sympathy. 'You must be worried sick about what's going to happen to your unit. He hasn't told me anything either, but I think there should be something in the local evening paper. The chief executive put out a statement to the local press ahead of the main news bulletin in tomorrow's national papers.'

'That's good to know.' Louise felt cheered by that. At least she wouldn't have too long to wait before she gained some inkling of what was to happen. 'I'll make sure that I buy a copy from the news kiosk when I leave here later on.'

As things turned out, it was a move that she soon began to regret. When her shift ended later that day she picked up a paper from the hospital news-stand on her way out and glanced briefly at the headlines.

Hospital Trust comes up with new solutions, she read. It appeared to be a fairly long article and, instead of reading it here and now, she tossed it onto the seat of her car, deciding that she would be able to study it more fully over supper.

Her supper turned to ashes in her mouth, though, as she read the journalist's report.

The Royal Forest Hospital will be designated a Centre of Excellence for the region, the Trust's management committee declared today.

Services at the hospital will be second to none, with specialist units equipped with state-of-the-art technology to cater for the needs of patients within the region.

Plans have been made to use the outpatients departments as centres where local GPs will see patients out of hours—including evenings and weekends. This will provide full cover for the neighbouring community.

In a separate measure, funding has been guar-

anteed for the Royal Forest Hospital's paediatric
A&E wing, thanks to provisions put in place by
its benefactor, the Ashleigh estate. An investment
trust has been set up to provide finance for years
to come. The new Lord Ashleigh stated, 'It was
my grandfather's abiding wish that the funding
would continue, and I'm pleased to say that the
paediatric A&E unit will continue to be supported
under new agreements that have been drawn up.

Louise slowly absorbed all that. Not only was James
funding the unit that was in contention with her own,
but also he had used her ideas to boost the Royal Forest
Hospital as a regional centre. Local GPs using outpatient facilities—hadn't she suggested that to him as a
means of supporting her own cause?

Seeing the words in print was like a betrayal that cut
to the heart. How could he have done that to her?

Looking back at the article, her gaze was drawn to
the last few lines.

Nothing has yet been stated about the future of
services at Castle Park Hospital. The paediatric
A&E unit is under threat of closure, with the
probability that the paediatric wards, maternity
and obstetric-gynaecology wards will also be
withdrawn. A spokesman for the Trust said, 'We
are still looking into the viability of keeping these
units open. Proposals will be put before a public
meeting to be held at the Town Hall on Saturday.'

She threw the paper down onto the table. Viability? What did that mean? It sounded very much as though her unit was in as much danger as ever. Had nobody listened to what she had been saying? Did the views of the parents whose children might have died if they hadn't been treated in her A&E department count for nothing?

James had given her a ray of hope when he'd suggested how she might turn the board around, but it had faded into oblivion when he'd used her ideas to further his own ends. He didn't care about helping her to keep what was as dear to her as if it were her own flesh and blood, no matter that it could save the lives of countless children, and he surely didn't care for her. If he had any feelings for her at all, how could he have stood back and let this happen?

She was still angry and bewildered when she went back to work the next morning. Nothing could take away the bitter taste in her mouth when she thought about what James had done, or failed to do. He was a member of the board, a well-respected man, and he could surely have swayed them to reconsider if he'd wanted to.

'I'm glad you've arrived,' Alice greeted her when she walked into the central area. 'It's been non-stop here for the last two hours. I was beginning to think we would need to call on agency staff to help out.'

'What's been happening?' Louise frowned. 'Not another traffic accident, surely? We've had a few of those lately.'

'More an influx of domestic accidents,' Alice said.

'And then there was a little boy who nearly drowned in the lake near to the country park. We managed to re-suscitate him, and he's in the observation ward now.'

'I'll go and take a look at him. How is he doing?'

'I think he'll be fine, given time. His heart rate was erratic for a while and his blood pressure was falling, but he started to mumble one or two words, so James is hopeful that there's no brain damage.'

'That does sound encouraging, at least.' She looked around. 'Is James with him now?' She wasn't at all sure that she was ready to face him just yet, but duty meant that she had to act in as professional a manner as was possible.

'No, he's with a two-month-old baby right now. The infant had a history of vomiting and diarrhoea over the last few days, and he appears to have gone into shock. The last I heard, James was struggling to put in an intra-venous line because the baby's circulation was closing down.'

That wasn't good news, and Louise glanced quickly at her list of patients before deciding that she could spare the time to go and see if he needed any help.

'I heard that you were having trouble,' she said as she went to stand beside him by the baby's cot. The infant wasn't moving, and showed no recognition that he knew anyone was there.

A glance at the monitor showed her that the baby's heart rate was over two hundred beats a minute and his blood pressure was extremely low. James was giving him one hundred per cent oxygen because, as the infant's circulation shut down, the oxygen would not be delivered to where it was needed. 'Is there anything that I can do?'

He glanced at her. 'You could do a blood glucose analysis for me. We're short on nurses this morning. I've put an intraosseous line into his left tibia, and I'm starting to infuse normal saline. His distal pulses are absent.'

'His blood glucose is only thirty,' Louise said. 'I'll treat that right away.'

James had infused the first bolus of saline, and now repeated with a second bolus. They waited to see if there was any change in the baby's condition.

'The heart rate's down a little,' James murmured after a while, 'but it's still high at one ninety. I'll give him a third bolus of fluid.'

Louise looked anxiously down at the infant. It was clear that the vomiting and diarrhoea had left him dehydrated, to such an extent that his life was in danger.

'He moved a finger just then,' James said, 'and his foot twitched slightly. I think we must be making some headway at last.' He glanced briefly at the monitor. 'His heart rate is down to one-fifty.'

'I think you've done it,' Louise said in a quiet tone. 'He's on the road to recovery.'

Her gaze meshed with his. 'Perhaps in a few months' time, when we're no longer able to accept patients here, and you're looking round your beautiful, well-equipped A&E unit at the Royal Forest Hospital, you'll remember this child, and the little boy whose windpipe was blocked, or even the child who nearly drowned today. Maybe you'll even feel a twinge of conscience that you did nothing to make sure that others like these had the same chance to cling on to life.'

He frowned, his gaze narrowing on her, but she didn't give him any opportunity to answer her because she turned away from the cot and walked out of the room.

For the next few hours she looked after the sick children in her care and tried to forget that he was anywhere near her. James, for his part, was kept busy with one patient after another and when lunch time came he left for a meeting with the Trust board.

Louise finished her shift and set off for home in the late afternoon. Coming back to Watermead House, with its fine gabled roof and backdrop of mature trees, usually had a calming effect on her, but today even the sight of the beautiful mellowed stone and latticed windows couldn't lift the burden of sorrow from her. The scent of roses drifted to her as she stood in the porch and put her key in the lock of the front door, but that didn't have its usual soothing power either.

She let herself into the house and walked slowly through to the kitchen. James was a wonderful man in many ways—a skilled doctor, a caring brother and grandson, a light-hearted, teasing saviour to all those children who depended on him for their lives. Yet he could be blind to the innermost needs of those closest to him. How could he not have seen what was happening to his brother? How could she love a man who had no understanding of her dearest hopes and dreams?

She flicked the switch on the kettle and then walked through to the oak-beamed lounge. The floor was finished in the same light oak, glowing softly with warm colour as the sunlight filtered through diamond-paned glass. In the centre of the room was a luxurious rug, woven from rich woollen fibres and shot through with shimmering threads of red, gold and green.

Two deep latticed windows looked out onto the garden beyond, and now Louise sat on the cushioned window-seat and gazed out at the trees that edged the lawn. This was her sanctuary, where she could watch the breeze gently lifting the leaves and all her troubles would miraculously melt away.

She sighed. That wasn't going to happen today. Turning back to look around the room, she saw the painting that Joseph had given to her and once again she marvelled at its beauty. Joseph had been a good man. He had done what he could to ensure that children would receive the treatment they needed at the Royal Forest Hospital, and it was only right that James would continue in his footsteps.

But why did it have to be at the expense of her unit? What would happen to her precious children in years to come?

The doorbell sounded and she stood up and braced herself to go and answer it. It was probably the man, delivering fresh fruit and vegetables from the farm further along the lane. She frowned. Hadn't he said he wouldn't be making his usual delivery until the weekend?

She opened the door, trying to summon up a smile and readying herself to exchange pleasantries with the man. Only it wasn't him at all. James was standing in her porch, admiring the pink rosebuds that peeped out from among the leafy branches that scrambled over the trellised arch.

'Good,' he said. 'I'm glad you're home. I was hoping that we might talk.'

She made a fairly good recovery from the shock of seeing him there, and lifted a brow. 'That's something new, isn't it? You don't seem to have been much in the mood for talking lately.'

'Life has been getting in the way,' he said. 'There were a lot of things I needed to get straight in my head, and several problems I had to sort out.'

'Yes, well, I dare say we all have problems of that sort at one time or another.'

He inclined his head a fraction to one side, as though he was studying her. 'I can see that you're still upset with me over something. Does that mean you're not going to invite me in?'

Over something? Her eyes narrowed on him. Did the man not know where he had gone wrong? She might not have expected him to be successful in swaying the board, but he might at least have made some attempt to help her out. She loved him, longed for him to tell her that he loved her in return, and all he could do was follow the management line. He had thrown her to the wolves.

'I suppose you had better come in, since you finally got around to deciding there was something to be said.' Her mouth flattened. 'I might as well hear you out.' She stood back and waved him through to the living room.

'Thanks. I appreciate that.' He smiled, ducking down to avoid the low entrance, and followed her along the hallway.

In the living room, he glanced around and admired the softly upholstered couch and ran his fingers over the antique writing desk that stood to one side of the armchair. 'This is lovely,' he murmured. 'I see you have a bureau with the same detailed carving. It's very intricate.'

'It is. I like it, so I searched the antique stores until I found what I wanted. I have some pieces with inlaid marquetry designs too. It's such an exquisite skill to lay in different layers of wood and form a satisfying pattern from them, I think.'

He nodded and turned to look at the picture of Watermead House, in pride of place on the wall beneath a gentle arch formed from the stonework. 'That's probably a very valuable piece, you know. I'm sure my grandfather knew that, and that's why he wanted you to have it.'

Her chin lifted. 'Perhaps he did, but it's not for sale. Your grandfather knew that its value was more than monetary. The picture's a representation of this house, and it will be forever a reminder of your grandfather's wonderful nature. I shall treasure it always.'

His mouth curved. 'I'm glad of that. I didn't mean

to imply that you should sell it. It simply occurred to me that you might want to have it insured at some point.'

'Perhaps I will.' Her tone was slightly mollified. 'If there's something you want to talk to me about, maybe you should sit down. I'll go and make some coffee.'

She waved a hand towards the couch and left the room briskly, hurrying along to the kitchen. She needed space, time alone so that she could catch her breath and adjust to the fact that he was here, in her house. He was so very normal, so much himself, when she was in pieces inside. She couldn't fathom what he was doing here.

Was he hoping to break the news to her before it appeared in the national papers that her A&E department was about to be shut down? Everything else in her world had gone wrong, so why not nudge the boulder and send the whole lot crashing down?

'Is there anything I can do to help?'

She pulled in a quick breath and whirled around to face him. 'No, thank you. I can manage.'

'If you say so, though I'm told I have a magic touch with coffee.' He sent her a crooked grin. 'It's all in the way you add the cream, you know, pouring it over the back of a spoon so that it lies on top.'

'Then, when you drink it, you get a milk moustache.' Despite her best efforts to remain cool with him she couldn't help herself. She stopped what she was doing and looked at him directly. 'You seem to be in a good mood,' she said. 'That's a little different from the way you've been acting these last few weeks. Has something happened? Has Robert come back?'

He nodded, and came to lean against the cupboards where she had laid out a tray. 'I sent him a few text messages, as you suggested, outlining the plans we have for the estate, and it seemed that he came to his senses at last. He came back last night. He wanted to go over everything with us and, from what I can gather, he's pleased with all the projects we have in mind.'

Her eyes widened. 'I'm really happy for you. What sort of things have you come up with?'

'Gemma's keen on having open days where we might have pageants and country fayres, and allow people to view the house and grounds. She was thinking of opening up her studio on those days and presenting some of her artwork for sale. She had it in mind to branch out into ceramics. Robert was particularly taken with your idea of expanding the stables. We thought we might use part of the estate to show how farming was carried out in years gone by, with the old horse and plough, and we want to restore some of the ancient machinery for people to view.'

Louise's mouth curved. 'I'm so glad that you're all happy with how you want to go on. It must be such a relief to have Robert back with you, and enthusiastic about what you want to do.'

'It is.'

She checked the percolator and began to pour the coffee into cups. 'Perhaps you'd better do your thing with the cream,' she said. 'Only I'll add my sugar first.'

'Will do.' He added a generous helping of cream to each cup, and then sent her an oblique glance. 'You were upset with me earlier today. When you had finished helping me with the boy who was suffering from dehydration, you made a comment about my having a twinge of conscience about the children who might not have the same chance in the future.'

Louise sipped her coffee, more to give herself time to compose herself than anything else. She carefully licked the cream from her upper lip and when she saw that his glance followed the movement she immediately regretted it. His eyes held that same arrested expression that they had when he'd held her in his arms and kissed her passionately. It was a man thing, a pure sexual drive, and it had nothing whatever to do with love, did it?

'I hoped you might come to realise that medicine is about more than creating super-hospitals and catering for needs on a large scale. There are individuals involved, people and children who are more than statistics, who will fall by the wayside if management has its way.' She pressed her lips together. 'But nothing has changed, has it? You still follow the management line.'

He studied her thoughtfully for a moment or two. 'I've learned a lot since I came back into clinical practice. It's made me think about why I put it on the back burner in the first place.'

She stared at him. 'And why was that?'

'Working in any branch of medicine, and especially with children, can be harrowing at times. I didn't want to find myself weighed down by the dark side of what goes on, when we're fighting overwhelming odds and nothing we do will make a difference. I needed to take a break and allow myself to recover from what can be a difficult, heartrending job. Then I decided that going into management and restricting my medical work to a few hours a week would be the answer.'

He made a rueful face. 'Neither of those alternatives did the trick. It was only when I started working alongside you that I felt as though I had finally found the right balance. Somehow, you showed me a different perspective, where I could learn to absorb the knocks and concentrate on the positive side of things. As you say, it's when the children recover and want your attention that you realise they're on the mend and you feel good inside. I still enjoy the management side of things, but from now on I'll work to achieve a better balance between the two.'

She stirred the cream into her coffee and took another sip. 'You had some success with the management side of things, didn't you? I read in the local paper about the funding for the Royal Forest Hospital. It must be cheering to know that your grandfather's dream is going to continue.' She frowned. 'I'm just not sure how you managed it, given that all your plans for the estate will take time to bring results.'

His mouth tilted at the corners. 'That all came about because of the roof repairs.'

She shook her head in confusion. 'I don't think I'm following you.'

'You remember that I told you I had to clear out the attic?'

She nodded.

'Well,' he went on, 'I spent some time doing that, and I discovered where all the paintings were that my grandfather had talked about—the paintings of the houses in Brooklea and various places round about. Some of them were in the old chapel, but a good many were up in the attic, and alongside them were several landscapes, portraits and silhouettes that my ancestors had collected over the years. There are far too many for us to ever put them up in the house, even if we alternated the collections over the years.'

Louise was intrigued. 'You said that my painting was valuable. Does that mean that you've had the others assessed?'

He nodded, and took time out to swallow his coffee. He didn't get one morsel of cream on his upper lip and she gave him a vexed looked. How did he do that?

He must have read her thoughts, because he laughed. 'Don't worry about it,' he murmured. 'It's very sexy when you do it.'

She glowered at him. 'You were telling me about the paintings,' she said.

'I had an art dealer take a look at them, and the figure he came up with was staggering. So I put it to Gemma and Robert that we had to decide what to do with them, and we made a list of those we would offer to the museums and art galleries in the region. Fortunately, they were mostly interested in buying them, so we've achieved two things—money to invest for the hospital fund and the upkeep of the estate, and a sale that will ensure the community has a chance to share in our heritage.'

'That's fantastic news. You must all be delighted.' She laid a hand on his arm, wanting to show him just how happy she was for him, but then she realised what she was doing and drew back from him.

'Why did you pull away from me?' he asked, looking at her curiously and beginning to move towards her. 'I like it when you touch me. I especially like it when you're close enough that I can hold you in my arms.'

She shook her head. 'I didn't get that impression when you sat with me out on the quadrangle. You seemed to change your mind and you moved away from me as though you had made a mistake.'

She was still backing away from him, but he followed her, winding his arms around her and capturing her as she came up against the corner cupboard. 'It was the wrong place and the wrong time, and there were people likely to intrude on us at any moment. Besides that, I knew how much you wanted to see your A&E unit secure for the future and we were at odds in everything we tried to do. It didn't seem right to take advantage of you when I might be the very person who could destroy everything you'd worked for.'

'And that's what happened, isn't it?' Her voice was barely a whisper. He was holding her so close to him that every part of her body was melded with his, and there was no way she could bear to look into his eyes just then. She loved him and wanted him, but he had chosen a path that took him away from her. She buried her face in the curve of his shoulder.

'No, Louise, that isn't true. I've been working all this time to persuade the board that your department needs to stay open. I've tried every argument I could think of. They've been inundated with petitions from parents and locals who are up in arms about the threat of closure. The MP for the region has added his two pennyworth, and I've given them a list of cost-cutting measures that we can put in place. They've had so much to think about that I'm surprised their heads aren't reeling.'

She looked up at him. 'You've done all that? I had no idea. Until you suggested ways I might sway them, I thought you were against keeping my unit open.'

'I couldn't bear to see it close. I know how much it means to you, and I've seen for myself how many children have survived because of it.' He stopped talking all at once and swooped to kiss her. It was a long, hard kiss, full of pent-up desire and passionate intensity, as though he would drown out any sense of denial that she might dredge up from the foggy depths of her mind.

Except her mind wasn't functioning at all just then. She was totally, utterly absorbed in that kiss, as though he had swept her off her feet and laid siege to every emotion she possessed. She wanted him, needed him, and couldn't bear for him to let her go.

'You have to know how hard it was for me to keep away from you,' he muttered against her cheek. 'I want you, Louise. I love you. I need you by my side.'

Love? Had he actually said it? She looked up at him, her eyes widening. 'You love me?'

'I love you.' He kissed her again, running his hands along her spine, smoothing his palms over her, as though he would know every inch of her. 'Do you think you could love me?'

She smiled up at him, her mouth soft and aching for his lips to claim hers once more. 'I can't help loving you,' she said huskily. 'I didn't want to, because it hurts so much to see everything I've worked for taken from me and dashed into the ground, but I love you anyway. I know now that you would have stopped it if you could.'

He rained kisses over her face, her throat, her mouth. 'But that's just it,' he said in a thickened voice. 'It won't come to that. I showed the board how the area needs your unit at its heart. With all the waterways close by, we get a high proportion of water-related accidents in this area, and that makes it all the more necessary for the A&E facilities to be within reach in the quickest possible time. There are also a couple of accident black spots not too far away and, until measures are put in place to counter that, we can't think of closing you down.'

She looked at him in shock. 'Have they agreed with you on this?'

He nodded. 'They have. You'll see it all in tomorrow's papers, but I wanted to be the first to tell you. I had confirmation this afternoon.'

'Oh, James…I can't tell you how that makes me feel. My heart's racing, I'm hot all over. I can't take it in. I'm so, so happy.' She didn't tell him that part of the reason she was feeling this way was because she was in his arms. That would confuse the issue altogether, wouldn't it?

'That's what I hoped you'd say.' He wrapped his arms even more tightly around her. 'But, most of all, I was hoping that you would agree to marry me. Will you marry me, Louise? Will you be my wife, and live with me and love me and be by my side for ever?'

'Oh, yes. Yes, please. I will. I love you.' She tilted her head upwards and pressed her mouth to his in a long and tender kiss. 'I love you so much.'

'That's good,' he said. 'It's such a relief to hear you say it, and perhaps now I'll be able to breathe again.' He smiled down at her. 'Did I tell you that I've set up an investment fund for your A&E unit? I wanted to make absolutely sure that there was no possibility of the board having a change of heart.'

'No, you didn't. I think I'm going to die of happiness,' she said in a choked voice. 'You are the most wonderful man that ever lived.'

'Really?' He made a crooked smile. 'I think that might be stretching it a bit, but if you want to go on kissing me and saying nice things, I'm all for it.'

'So am I,' she said on a chuckle. 'You make my whole body tingle.'

'Me too,' he murmured, bending his head and kissing her soundly until the world began to spin and her head was filled with cotton wool clouds. 'I love you, Louise, more than anything, and I want to spend my life with you. You're my very special angel.'

Passion. Power. Suspense.
It's time to fall under the spell
of Nora Roberts.

For the latest script of his blockbuster horror film, Nash Kirkland tracks down self-proclaimed witch Morgana Donovan and sceptically demands the secrets of her imaginary craft.

Nash is stunned to discover that he is equally mystified by and attracted to Morgana. Either he is being driven mad or Morgana is telling the truth about her powers. And the most important choice Nash will ever make depends on getting the answer right.

This is the first volume in Nora Roberts' spellbinding *The Donovan Legacy*.

Available 2nd January 2009

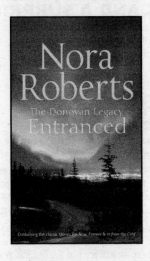

FREE

4 BOOKS AND A SURPRISE GIFT!

We would like to take this opportunity to thank you for reading this Mills & Boon® book by offering you the chance to take FOUR more specially selected titles from the Medical™ series absolutely FREE! We're also making this offer to introduce you to the benefits of the Mills & Boon® Book Club™—

★ **FREE home delivery**
★ **FREE gifts and competitions**
★ **FREE monthly Newsletter**
★ **Books available before they're in the shops**
★ **Exclusive Mills & Boon Book Club offers**

Accepting these FREE books and gift places you under no obligation to buy; you may cancel at any time, even after receiving your free shipment. Simply complete your details below and return the entire page to the address below. You don't even need a stamp!

YES! Please send me 4 free Medical books and a surprise gift. I understand that unless you hear from me, I will receive 6 superb new titles every month for just £2.99 each, postage and packing free. I am under no obligation to purchase any books and may cancel my subscription at any time. The free books and gift will be mine to keep in any case.

M9ZEE

Ms/Mrs/Miss/Mr...Initials ....
BLOCK CAPITALS PLEASE

Surname ....

Address ....

....

....Postcode ....

Send this whole page to:
The Mills & Boon Book Club, FREEPOST CN81, Croydon, CR9 3WZ